No Matter the Distance

CINDY BALDWIN

No Matter the Distance

Quill Tree Books
An Imprint of HarperCollinsPublishers

Library of Congress Cataloging-in-Publication Data
Names: Baldwin, Cindy, author.
Title: No matter the distance / Cindy Baldwin.
Description: First edition. | New York, NY : Quill Tree Books, [2023] |
    Audience: Ages 8-12. | Audience: Grades 4-6. | Summary: The unexpected
    appearance of a dolphin in her backyard creek helps a sixth-grader with
    cystic fibrosis learn to write her own story.
Identifiers: LCCN 2022008240 | ISBN 9780063006447 (hardcover)
Subjects: CYAC: Novels in verse. | Cystic fibrosis—Fiction. |
    Identity—Fiction. | Dolphins—Fiction. | Loss—Fiction. | Family
    life—North Carolina—Fiction. | LCGFT: Novels in verse.
Classification: LCC PZ7.5.B35 No 2023 | DDC [Fic]—dc23
LC record available at https://lccn.loc.gov/2022008240

Typography by Laura Mock
23 24 25 26 27 LBC 5 4 3 2 1

First Edition

For
Megan Murray, James Lawlor, Melissa Moore,
and every other CF friend who has helped me through the
difficult days—

And in memory of Kristi.
With each year our daughters grow, I miss you.

spring break

SIXTH GRADE

By halfway through the year
I'm used to the changes
of sixth grade:
no more all-day
elementary school classroom
with my name
taped to a desk.
Now I have
a schedule to remember,
a locker combination,
a different teacher every hour.

But some things
are just the same as last year,
like the way the whole school
buzzes with electric energy
the day before spring break.

THE ASSIGNMENT

In English class
Ms. Berman gives us the assignment
ten minutes before the final bell.
"During the last week of school in June," she says,
"we'll be holding a sixth-grade poetry slam.
Any sixth grader who wants
may submit a poem to the committee,
and the winners will have the chance
to read their poem at an assembly
for the whole sixth grade."

Every cell inside me
goes quiet, like Ms. Berman's words
are a cool, clean waterfall across my skin.
I can almost *hear* the whisper
of the battered notebook
filled with poems I've written
stuffed inside my backpack.

"The theme for the poetry slam
is What I Know About Myself," Ms. Berman says.
"In your poems, we want you to explore
who you are—not just the things

anyone can see, but the things that make you *you*,
deep inside yourself.
The deadline for submissions
will be two weeks after spring break ends.
        Class
                dismissed."

The room erupts—chairs
scraping back against the floor,
the flurry of students hurrying out
into the April sunshine.
But I sit still, glued into my chair
by the glittering promise
Ms. Berman has just laid out in front of me.
A poem. My poem. For the whole sixth grade.

BLANK SLATE

Cricket finds me after class
and we watch for our bus—
   together,
    just like always,
her backpack
full of seventh-grade textbooks
bumping against her spine.

Cricket is pretty much
a genius
and so she gets put
into all the advanced classes
even though
she's in sixth grade
   just like me.

Sometimes,
I envy Cricket's brain,
how easily it seems
to make sense of the world.
Mine feels the opposite:
   like every day I grow,
   I only get less clear

on what it means
to be Penny Rooney.

Cricket's known
forever
what she wants:
to work for NASA—
put her great brain to work
       like Katherine Johnson,
       the mathematician
who charted the course
for the rocket
that reached the moon.

Next to Cricket,
I feel like a blank slate,
still figuring out
where I fit
in the puzzle
       of school,
       my family,
       the world
full of people
who seem to know
exactly what it is
that lights them up.

Cricket moved in next door
in second grade.
Her real name is Christine,
like her grandma,
>   but her parents
>   call her Cricket
>   for her cheerful,
>   chirping chatter.

Cricket's mama
brought casserole after casserole
the year I took all those trips
to the hospital
so Mama didn't have to cook.
We may be different
but we fit together perfectly.
Cricket's been my best friend
so long, sometimes
>   I don't know
>   where she ends
>   and I begin.

NOTEBOOK

On the bus

    I pull out
    my poetry notebook,
        open to
        a fresh new page,
            and try to write
            Ms. Berman's poem.

WHAT I KNOW ABOUT PENNY ROONEY

These are the things
I know about Penny Rooney.

Small girl, all bones
and points, with brown hair and eyes.

Black-framed glasses
that always fall too far down my nose.

Poems that simmer and seethe
under my skin, begging to come out—

but never sound quite the way
I hoped they would once they're written.

Not so good at math.
Numbers always tangle in my brain.

A girl with lungs that don't
always breathe the way they should.

Why does it seem like I could write
what I know about Cricket
or *what I know*
about my parents or my sister
a hundred times better
than what I know about myself?

MY SISTER

Liana is already home
when I get off the bus.
Her voice echoes

from the music room
when I step inside the house.
I once heard someone say,

*Liana sings
like she's giving you
her whole soul,*

and she really does.
Right now she's learning
a solo from a sad musical,

bittersweet and beautiful—
the kind of music that wraps
its fingers round your heart.

If I were to write a poem—

What I Know About Liana

—this music would be first.

BANANA BREAD

Mama's at the kitchen table,
phone pressed to her ear,
calendar pages spread in front of her.
Most days Mama gets home before I do,
but getting home isn't the same
as getting off work.
Mama is a secretary
at my old elementary school.
Daddy says she runs the place.
They'd go under without you, Liz.

There's a loaf of banana bread on the counter,
the kind Mama makes sometimes
full of so much butter and cream cheese
I need extra digestive enzymes.
I cut a slice and sit down at the bar,
shake the enzyme pills
into my hand.
I have to take them every time I eat—
just another part
of *cystic fibrosis*,
the disease I've got twisted
into the double helix of my DNA.

With CF, your pancreas gets all blocked up,
so the chemicals that break down your food
end up stuck in traffic.
Instead, they give you pills made of *pig* enzymes
      (which is kind of gross)
to help digest everything you eat.
High-fat foods need more, to break down
all that deliciousness.

Liana finishes her practice
and plops into a chair beside me.
"What's up, Buttercup?" she says, bumping
her shoulder into mine. Liana is always giving me
ridiculous nicknames, because when she was a freshman
she took one year of French
and decided everyone should call each other things
like *my duck* or *my sweet bun*,
the way the French do.
"You excited for spring break?"

"Yeah," I say,
feeling that electric buzz in my fingertips again.
I think of telling her about Ms. Berman's poem—
about the sixth-grade poetry slam
and what I know about Penny Rooney,
but something stops me.

What would Liana say she knows about me?
What would Liana say she knows about herself?

Maybe everyone else in the world
is walking around
sure of exactly who they are,
deep inside their skin.

Maybe I'm the only blank-slate girl
still wondering where I fit in.

THE CREEK

"Come on," Liana says
when we've finished
our snack. "Let's go swim."

"Going to the creek,"
Liana calls to Mama.
"We'll be back soon."

We run upstairs,
grab our swimsuits.
And in two blinks—

We're outside,
the whole beautiful
spring-break world around us.

Blue sky stretched overhead,
the sharp scent
of creek—grass—mud.

The lap of water
as we run past the kayak shed
and the creek comes into view.

"Race you!" Liana shouts
before we're even at the dock,
kicking off her flip-flops.

By the time she hits
the water, I've got
my shoes and glasses off.

I follow her in,
arms arrowing as I dive
through the cool water.

My brain is clear
of anything except
stroke, kick, breathe

as I come out of my dive
and start to freestyle.
I count my breaths:

Left—breathe in—
stroke—blow out—
right—breathe in—repeat.

I think of Mama
and all the times
she's helped me practice,

day after day last summer
until I could swim fast enough
to *almost* make up for being short

and having puny lungs.
Even with all that practice,
tall Liana—

her lungs strong
and ordinary—
usually wins our races.

But today—today,
I get there first,
filled with bubbly sunshine.

When you are not just
a little sister, but
a *little* little sister

whose medical chart
says things like
failure to thrive,

beating a big sister

just
      feels
           good.

WHAT WE SEE NEXT

We're halfway back across the creek—
not racing now—
when Liana grabs my arm
hard enough to pull me under.
She drags me back up
as I choke and splutter,
but doesn't let go.
I can feel her feet churning the water
so we'll stay afloat.

"Pen," she hisses, "swim back
to the dock
     as quick
          as you can, but—

please   *don't*   *splash.*"

I have no idea what's going on,
what made Liana's fingers
grip so tight,
her voice hiss with nerves.
But for maybe the first time ever,
I do exactly what she says.

We breaststroke back to shore,
pull ourselves up onto the dock,
skin tingling in the suddenly frigid April air.

"Okay," I say, trying to stop
my teeth chattering.
I put my glasses on but still can't see
whatever it was that made Liana freeze.

The moment stretches

     thin
     and
     tense—

But Turtle Creek looks the same
as always: calm and wide
and lazy, swirling past so slow
you hardly see it move.

"I saw something," Liana says,
still a little shaken.
"A fin. Not too far away
from where we were."
Her words sizzle into me.

Nobody I know
has ever *personally* seen
a bull shark in our creek—
not here, a mile inland
from the big Neuse River.
But everyone knows the stories:
the fishermen who claim their catch
disappeared mid-reel, stolen
by a monster from the deep.
Or the scientists who came
last year, to study sharks
who swim in brackish rivers,
and tagged *three* in creeks like ours.
Pictures were all over Facebook
when that happened,
and Mama made us promise
to hightail it out of the water
if we ever saw something suspicious.

But we never have.

    We wait
    for a long breath.

Then Liana points and waves.
"See?" she cries. "Right there!

It's gray. Look—in the middle,
between our dock and Cricket's."

I squint at the denim water,
stare so hard my eyes sting.
The creek is smooth as glass.
And then suddenly,
between one breath
and the next:

    I see it.

A pewter dorsal fin, slicing
up into the chilly springtime air.

IN MY BACKYARD

"Hang on," Liana says
as the fin sinks out of sight.
"Is that . . ."
I keep my eyes trained hard
on the place it disappeared.
"Yeah," I say, knowing
what Liana's asking
the way sisters sometimes do.
"It rolled." And almost
before I've finished speaking

the

dorsal

fin is back,

catching sun

like polished marble,

silver water   glistening

on luminous   gray skin.

Shark fins? They don't roll like that.
If they ever break the surface—
which is rare—
they glide, smooth and steady.

The creature rises farther
from the water, and it's clear now:
the broad, smooth back,
round head, graceful tail.

"Whoa," I breathe.
The wonder of it fills me up
like a helium balloon.
Here we are, in our dripping suits,
seeing something maybe
nobody has seen before.

  A dolphin.
  In Turtle Creek.

The creek I fell into at age four.
The creek where I first learned to swim.
The creek we fish and kayak.
The creek isn't quite freshwater—
holding the memory of the sea
with its tides and salt—
but it's nearly fifty miles
from the open ocean.

  A dolphin.
  Right there, in *our* creek.

And for the first time
since school got out, I'm not thinking
about Ms. Berman or poems
or what I don't know about Penny Rooney.
I'm thinking of nothing
at all, except the glimmer of light
on that shining fin

      as a *dolphin* swims lazily
      through my own backyard.

TELLING MAMA

Mama's at the back door
when Liana and I run up,
breathing hard and fast.
"How was the water?" Mama asks.
"Perfect." Liana smiles
the smile that got her voted
Homecoming Queen last year,
the smile that makes you smile right back.

"Guess what we saw?" I blurt,
words tripping over each
other in their hurry to be said.
"A dolphin. We saw a dolphin!
Swimming in the creek.
It was beautiful. Like—"
I pause. No metaphor I've
ever learned in English class
could do that moment justice.
"It was amazing, Mom," Liana says.

Mama's forehead wrinkles.
"Really?" she asks, doubt swirled
through her voice like eddies
in the water. "Are you sure, girls?

It wasn't just a fish?"
I've never been so sure of anything
in my whole life. I nod.
"Positive," I say. Liana backs me up.

"Huh," says Mama, the little crease
of doubt still tucked into her face.
"Well, come inside now.
You'll both need to shower
and put away your clean laundry
before Daddy's home for dinner.
Maybe don't swim this week—
just in case."

Mama's words are like river stones,
settling heavy in my stomach,
smothering the bright wonder
of the dolphin cutting
through the water.

Liana and I trail silently into the house.
She gets into the shower first,
the rush of water hissing
through the bathroom pipes,
        leaving me cold
                and waiting.

DOUBT

The afternoon crawls by, slow
as honey sliding from a jar.
Liana disappears
back into the practice room
and I hear her singing warm-ups,
her steady voice moving patiently
through *vee-vay-vah-voe-voo*

      again,

      again,

      again,

preparing for her senior recital
next month.

I sit outside, try to write a poem
about the dolphin we saw,
but every moment it seems fainter
in my memory—
like maybe Liana and I
made the whole thing up.

WHAT I KNOW ABOUT DADDY

Daddy comes home in time for dinner
and heads upstairs
to shower like he does
after work each day, to keep
the hospital germs away from me.
He comes out smelling of soap,
hair slick and wet,
and gives us all gigantic hugs.
"Spring break, huh, Lucky Penny?"
he says, spinning me around
like I'm still three years old.

This is what I know about my daddy:
He's like a bear, all brown beard
and gruff voice,
with a round belly and soft arms
that help him give the *best* hugs.
He always says he has a brain *like a steel trap*
and it's true—Daddy's great
with numbers and remembering,
and his clever tongue makes the funniest jokes.

He's a respiratory therapist,
spending his days at the hospital making sure
      patients have enough oxygen,
        the ventilators in the ICU work,
        anyone who needs breathing treatments
          gets them.
At first he was a nurse—
but after I was born, he went back to school
to learn as much as he could
about how lungs work, and how
            to keep
               them working.

BEFORE DINNER

I corner Daddy, ask him,
"Have you ever heard
of dolphins in our creek?"

Daddy frowns
in confusion.
"Dolphins in Turtle Creek?"

he asks, pointing a thumb
out the window
where the stream tickles

the edge of our backyard.
"Can't say as I have,"
he says.

"Though you know
they always say
there might be

sharks out there,
once in
a blue moon."

"I don't mean them,"
I say, but I remember
the skeptical look

on Mama's face
this afternoon—
so I let the subject go,

swim away from us
just like that dolphin
disappeared downstream.

DOLPHIN DREAMING

That night
I dream
of the dolphin.
She swims
through pools
of moonlight,
water droplets
beading
on her rubber skin.
In my dream,
I can feel
the water slide
across my arms,
light as a feather's
kiss, warm
as summer rain.
We swim together,
the dolphin
and I, and just
when I know
I'm on the verge
of waking,
the dolphin

surges up
through the water
and leaps
into the air,
moonlight catching
on her gray
back, turning
it diamond-bright
for one shining,
shimmering
second before
plunging
back into the water.

As the splash
washes over me,
something else
does too:
a feeling, burning
into my mind
the way falling stars
leave tracks
as they blaze
across the sky—
something
wordless

but strong
as the feel
of my daddy's hugs
or the scent
of Mama baking.

Before she swims
away, the dolphin
turns a circle
around me, and
I swear
by the way her
permanent grin
splits her face,
she feels
it too.

WAKING

When I wake
the next morning, I'm filled
with the remembered joy
of that dream—
but also a question
that crackles through my brain:
How did I know
to call the dolphin *she*?

MORNING ROUTINE

My morning routine
goes like this:
wake up, get dressed,
brush teeth, swallow
my empty-stomach pills

      (they're different
      from the huge handful
      I take with breakfast later)

then curl up
in my favorite
floofy armchair,
the one so old
and saggy Mama
always threatens to chuck it.

      (But she never will
      because she knows
      I love it so.)

Twice a day—more if I'm sick—
this is where I do
my breathing treatments.

I pull my favorite blanket
over my legs—
the one my parents have had
almost as long
as they've had me,
woven through
with purple roses, with
Someone I Love
Has Cystic Fibrosis
along the bottom.

> (A long time ago,
> the story goes,
> there was a kid with CF
> who couldn't say *cys-tic fi-bro-sis*
> so instead, he called it
> *sixty-five roses*,
> which sounds almost the same.
> Ever since,
> purple roses mean CF.)

I start with the nebulizer:
a little machine
with a loooooooooong tube
and a mouthpiece on the end,
like a teacup
made by aliens.
I put the medicine in the cup
and plug it into the tube,
and voilà—
air pushes out:

from the machine
            through the tube
                    to the alien teacup,

and the liquid medicine
becomes mist.
When I put the mouthpiece
between my teeth
and breathe in, all that misty medicine
is pulled into my lungs—
and when I breathe out, the mist
wreathes around my head.

I do four nebulizer medications
in a row—

four squirts
from little plastic vials:

One to open my airways
when they want to clamp closed.

One to break down
all the nasty,
sticky mucus
filling up my lungs.

One that's just really, really
salty water,
because it helps
keep things hydrated.

The last, an antibiotic,
misted right into my lungs
to fight the germs
that call them home.

With the mouthpiece clamped
between my teeth,
I strap on my vest.
Imagine a life vest,
except it has

a motor inside
that shakes and shakes
and shakes,
to clear my airways out
and keep me from drowning
in my own lungs.
People always ask
if it feels
like a massage, but it doesn't.

It doesn't feel like much
of anything, when you're
as used to it as I am.

ONE OF THE LUCKY ONES

All my life
people have said,
You're so lucky.

Sometimes it's a doctor
the first time they meet me—
I go in for a flu shot
or a strep test,
and when they learn I have CF
their eyes get round.
You look so healthy! they say,
and *I* know
the only things *they* know
about CF
are from one page of a textbook
back in 1981
about how CFers live
        short

            sick

                lives.

Sometimes it's my CF team—
Dr. Theo with her neat gray hair,

Nurse Jen with her colorful scrubs,
the RTs and PTs and RDs
>   (*respiratory* therapists
>   and *physical* therapists
>   and *registered dieticians*)
who I see every three months
at the Duke University Hospital
Pediatric CF Clinic
two hours away.
They tell me, *Lucky girl!*
when they see
my pulmonary function tests
or congratulate me
on going so long without a hospital stay.

If I'm coughing or my lungs hurt
or I'm just tired
from the long drive out to Durham,
Dr. Theo or Nurse Jen
will remind me of their other patients,
the ones with
>   feeding tubes,
>   port-a-caths,
>   lung transplants.

All my life
people have said,
You're so lucky—
and I know it's true.

The life expectancy for a CF patient
wasn't even forty when I was born
and now it's all the way to fifty—
there are medications I can take
that didn't exist a few years ago,
ones that help all my faulty genes
work a little better.

Every year, the future gets
　　　brighter
　　　clearer
　　　luckier
for people like me.

A TON OF BRICKS

Way back
when people sat around
stuffing the English language full of idioms,
somebody once compared surprises
to a ton of bricks
that fly out of the sky
and thump you, *boom*,
when you're least expecting it.

I'm not expecting
to be hit with a ton of bricks
when the house phone rings
after breakfast
and Mama calls out,
Penny, it's for you,
and I hear Cricket's voice
on the other end.
She talks through tears—
Penny, my parents just told me
my dad got offered a new job
and we're moving to Virginia
as soon as school is done.

I'm not expecting bricks from the sky
on the first real morning
of a perfect spring break—
but the thing about bricks is
they don't really wait
for you to be ready
before they fall.

SORRY

Mama hugs me, says,
"I'm so sorry, Penny,"
tells me about her best friend

when she was my age, how
they kept in touch
when Mama's family moved away.

Daddy says I'd better
practice keeping my room clean,
so there will be space

on the floor for Cricket
to sleep when she comes
back to visit.

Liana doesn't say anything,
just hugs me
and puts Broadway music on loud

and grabs my hands
so I'll dance around with her,
which is what my sister always does

when she's feeling down.
They help, those hugs
and *sorry*s and dance parties,

but it still feels
like there's a new hole
inside of me.

What I know about Penny Rooney:
a blank-slate girl
whose best friend is moving

far, far away.

PENNY WITHOUT CRICKET

I go up to my bedroom
and try to write
a poem to give Ms. Berman

for the poetry slam—
but I can't.
The words don't come.

How can I explain
what I know
about Penny Rooney

if Cricket moves away?
In third grade
one teacher called us

Cricket'n'Penny,
like it was all one word.
A package deal.

Sixth grade ends
in less
than two months.

What will
Cricket'n'Penny be
with one half gone?

THE DOLPHIN

All day long,
my thoughts ricochet
between Cricket
and that dolphin.
My real-life memories
of the dolphin tangle
together with my dream
until I can't be sure
what really happened,
and what was just
a dream. It was so vivid,
I swear I could tell you
exactly how it feels
to swim next to her,
to have the water
from her wake wash
over your head,
even though yesterday
I was out of the creek
before I even saw her.

I have never been
the kind of person

who does big, brave things.
That's more Cricket,
or Liana—both of them
dive into life with hands
outstretched, ready
to grab whatever comes
and never let it go.
If she hadn't thought
our dolphin was a shark,
I bet Liana would've stayed.
But me? I wouldn't think so—
except that in my dream
I *swam* with the dolphin,
joyful and unafraid.

DOING THE DISHES

That night, Liana and I
load the dinner dishes
into the dishwasher.
She puts on a playlist
and we sing along together,
which has always been
our thing.
Last year, we sang
Liana's favorite Taylor Swift song
at a talent show
and practiced so many times
even Mama and Daddy
learned every single word.
When Liana and I sing duets
I count every breath
thanks to CF.
My throat aches. Head spins.
But Liana's voice
makes the world around me
feel wonderful and wide.

"Do you think
that dolphin will be back?"

I ask when I'm tired out
from singing.
Liana shrugs.
"I doubt it," she says,
scrubbing lasagna cheese
from a dinner plate.
"I mean, have you
ever heard of dolphins
so far from the sea?
I know they see them
sometimes
in the Neuse,
but never, ever here."
I think how far
the dolphin must've swum
to get to our backyard.

"It was cool, though,
right?" I say, when what
I really want to ask is:
It was real, though, right?
Liana smiles.
"The coolest thing
I've ever seen, Butter Bean,"
and then she flicks me
with her dishwater hands,

droplets of soapy wet
landing all over my face
and shirt. And before
I can take another breath,
we're in a water fight,
our giggles getting louder
and louder, rising
to the ceiling
until Mama finally comes
to investigate and throws
her hands up in the air
and yells at us to please
clean up the dishes
and the extra mess
we've made, before
she decides to sell us
to the circus.

PENNY, CURIOUS

Later, once Liana and I are both
clean and dry
and all the dishes are done,
I bite down
on my first nebulizer, press go
on the vest, pull Mama's laptop
onto my lap.
Mama always says I was born
into the world as a person
who wanted to know things.
I guess that's one thing I could say
I know about Penny Rooney:
always curious.
While Daddy and Liana play Scrabble
at the kitchen table
and Mama sits cross-legged
reading on the couch,
I open up a browser and search:
Dolphins in Turtle Creek
Havelock, North Carolina.
The only thing that comes back
are a bunch of hits
about dolphin-watching

up in New Bern,
where the wide Neuse River
flows through town.
There's a bunch of videos
of Hurricane Florence in 2018,
when the rivers leapt their banks
and flooded all our houses—
everything so changed
that dolphins swam
through Havelock and New Bern
for days. But no matter
how hard I look, there's nothing
at all about dolphins in my creek
or any other like it.

When I pause my machines
to change to my next nebulizer,
Mama looks up from her book.
"You're awfully focused over there,"
she says. "What are you working on?"
I shrug, remembering
the doubtful look she gave us
when Liana and I told her about the dolphin.
I wish I had the words to explain
how ever since
that moment, I can't get it

out of my brain.
"Have you ever had something happen
that seemed impossible?"
I say at last.
Mama laughs, like whatever she'd
expected me to say, that wasn't it.
She smiles and says,
"So *many* impossible things."

MAMA AND ME

Mama comes over and squeezes
into the recliner next to me.
It's a tight fit these days—
only possible
because I'm what my parents
politely call *petite*, thanks to CF
sucking all the nutrition out of me.
I'm not like Daddy,
who's soft and fluffy,
or like Liana, who's tall and big,
with round arms and curvy hips.
Even Mama, who's on
the smaller side herself,
isn't shaped the way I am.
The only part of me that isn't bones
is my belly, which Mama calls
a *CF tummy*—awkward and bulging,
another side effect of messed-up
digestion. It didn't bother
me until I turned eleven
and started to notice
how all the other girls at school
are starting to have

more roundness up high, and less
down low—except for me.
Mama got me a pair
of training bras last year,
but there's nothing there
to fill them yet.

Mama tucks her arm around me
and pulls me close, not caring
that my vest shakes us both.
She leans over to plant a kiss
on top of my hair.
"Penny Elizabeth Rooney,
you and your sister
are my very favorite impossible things."
And I know she's going to tell me
the same story she's told my whole life.
But even though I sometimes
roll my eyes when she gets started
and say, *I know, I know already*,
secretly, deep down,
I love it. So I say nothing, keep
the nebulizer between my teeth,
and snuggle deeper into the chair.

IMPOSSIBLE THINGS

This is the story Mama tells:
>A million years
>or so ago
Mama and Daddy met
at a coffee shop
>where she was
>a barista
and he was on his lunch break
from the hospital, where he'd
just started his brand-new job.
Daddy says he fell in love
>at first sight
>of the sparkle
>in Mama's eyes
when she wrote his name—
Steve Rooney—
on his hot chocolate cup.
>*No lattes for you?*
>she asked.
Daddy shook his head
and smiled his jolly
Santa Claus smile
and said nope,

he didn't drink coffee,
        but he was *obsessed*
        with hot chocolate.

So they got married
        (eventually)
and moved into an apartment
with leaky pipes, and pretty soon
        they decided
        to have a baby.
Except for some people, you have
to do more than just decide—
and that's how it was for them.
Two years passed, and no baby came
and so they went to the kind of doctor
who helps with things like that,
        and finally,
        Liana was born.

"Liana was our first impossible thing,"
Mama says now, smoothing
my hair over my head where her kiss lies.
I know the next part
        as well as I know
        the sound of my own name.
When Liana started school,

Mama and Daddy decided their family
wasn't done, so they went back
to the baby doctor.

And finally, *I* was born.

"That was the start of our second
impossible thing," Mama says.
My stomach tightens,
knowing what comes next.
This part of the story
still echoes
in the way my parents look at me
when I get a cold,
or the pollen count
starts me sneezing out
my brains.
They think I don't see it,
the way the worry thoughts float
along the edges of everything
when I get sick, but I do.

"You were so cute when you were born,"
says Mama with a smile.
"Such a fat little thing, with all that hair.
You were like a baby from TV,

pink-skinned, rosebud mouth,
all of it. We were so happy."

    Mama pauses,
    and the twist
    in my stomach
    grows.

"Then I got sick," I say, when
she doesn't finish the story.
Mama nods. "Then you got sick."
You can see it
in our family photo albums:
how the fat baby that was me
    turned gaunt and bony
    and cried all the time.
How suddenly the pictures
were taken in hospital rooms, with plastic
tubes coming out of my nose and arms.
"You stopped eating," Mama says quietly.
"You threw up. All the time.
And then, when we got
the newborn
test results back . . ."
"I had CF," I say.
I've known the ending of this story
for my whole life.

"Things got bad for a while there,"
says Mama. I can see
the memory of all that badness
        etched in the lines
        around her mouth.
"One night, the doctor told us
you might not make it
through the week."
"But I did," I say, because
it's how the story goes.
"You did," Mama says. "You grew strong
and finally started eating again
and turned into a fierce and feisty toddler.

        And that, Penny,
        was my third
        impossible
        thing."

WHAT I KNOW ABOUT PENNY ROONEY, PART 2

An impossible girl
with an impossible story
and a family who loves her
impossibly much.

Except—
I don't remember
the tubes or the hospital
or the almost dying.
Mama and Daddy
and Liana tell stories
about it—but stories
are all they are to me.

Our house is full of pictures:
Baby Liana, fair-haired
and smiling.
Liana older, hair darker now,
graduating preschool.
Liana with baby Penny.
Even a few of Mama and Daddy
at the hospital with me,
their faces pale and tired.

There are pictures, too,
of us older:
Me and Cricket on the dock
on a warm summer day.
Liana and Daddy, dirt-streaked
and grinning
in front of a tent
on one of their
beloved overnight kayak trips,
which I can never go on
because there's no electricity
to run my nebulizer
and no room in a kayak
to store all the things I need.

Our house is full of stories
about the Rooney family—
about lovely Liana
and Lucky Penny,
Mama's best impossible things.

But who exactly
is Penny Rooney on her own?

I think Ms. Berman
and the poetry committee
want more than just a bunch
of family stories I've been told.
After all, Ms. Berman said
What I Know About Myself,
not What Other People Tell Me
About Who I Am.

It's funny, how even the things
I think I know about myself
end up being more about
         my family
                  in the end.

MIRACLES

The next morning at church
Sister Monroe gives a talk about miracles.
An extraordinary event
you can't explain, she says, *but it's still real.*
I sit between Mama and Liana
and think about miracles and impossible things,
about Cricket moving
and a dolphin in my own backyard.
I tug at the ear loops
of the purple-rose-patterned mask Mama
always makes me wear to church
to protect me from everyone's coughs and sniffles
and remember what Mama said last night:
that *I* was one of her impossible things.
My birth, me growing strong and fierce—
those were miracles for her and Daddy,
extraordinary events, impossible
challenges overcome, magic dipped into their lives.

Maybe if I prayed for a miracle
Cricket's parents wouldn't want to leave.

BETTER THAN SISTERS

Cricket's waiting on our front step
when we get home from church.
Her shoulders slump.
Mama hugs her on her way inside,
Liana and Daddy both say
they're sorry about the move,
and then it's just the two of us
left on the front step.
We sit side by side, shoulders touching.
"I guess Virginia's not so far,"
Cricket says finally.
"Mom says it's only four hours by car."

      Four hours is a galaxy away
      compared to next door.

Cricket clears her throat. "Mom says
maybe next summer I can come back,
spend a couple weeks with you."

      Next summer is a hundred years away
      compared to now.

"You're the only sister I've ever had,"
says Cricket, who has two noisy brothers instead.
"Not sisters," I say, because even though
I love Liana, Cricket's something different.
I wrap my pinky through hers and squeeze.
"Something better than just sisters.
Like two petals on a flower
or two halves of a cracked egg."

Liana may be the sister I was born with,
the sister I'll always
love and look up to—
but Cricket is the sister I chose.

THE VISITOR

Monday afternoon
I'm on the dock,
swirling my feet

in Turtle Creek
as it streams
slowly past,

my notebook next to me—
untouched.
No more hints about

what I might know
about Penny Rooney
fill the clean pages.

And then I see it,
from the corner of my eye:
a splash downstream,

a flash of silver-gray,
an arcing fin
cutting through the water.

My breath stops
as the moment tingles
on my skin

and the memories
of what we saw Friday
rush right back.

I don't breathe
for what feels like
a hundred years,

until I see it again—
there! Clear as day,
the dorsal fin

followed by a playful
splashing tail
sending diamond droplets

sparkling
through the sunshine.
I stay still as stone,

watching so hard
my eyes start to hurt,
until the dolphin surfaces

again a moment later.
Closer this time.
It's no farther from me

than the length
of the swimming pool
at the rec center.

This time, when she rolls
her body out of the water,
I can see her whole

round smooth
shining head
breaking the surface.

The air around me
seems to *hum*
with electricity,

like the feeling you have
when you're trying
to go to sleep

the night before
your birthday.
I watch and watch

as the dolphin swims
and plays—
gliding in and out

of the water,
splashing her tail,
once even rolling

over, so for a second
I can see
her flapping pectoral fins.

Slowly, slowly,
she closes the distance
to my dock.

And even though
I've never been the kind
of girl who does big, brave things—

seeing the dolphin
here, in my creek, again,
does something to my heart.

I'm not supposed
to swim alone
but right now I don't care.

Mama and Liana are inside.
Daddy—who doesn't work Mondays—
is weeding the front yard.

No one can see me
right here
sitting on the dock.

I pull off my glasses,
strip down to my shorts
and sports bra

and slip off the dock,
feeling the cool silk
of the water close around me.

I bob up and shake
wet hair from my eyes,
treading water,

and wait
as the dolphin
comes closer.

HERE IN THE WATER

I can see that she is *huge*—
longer than a grown-up man is tall.
A zing of nervousness
flicks through me
as she swims ever closer.
I can hear Mama's voice
in my head—
Girl, what do you think you're doing?
But something inside me
is stronger
than the fear. I stay,
legs windmilling the water,
arms pulling in little circles,
my heart
ten sizes too big
for my chest.
When the dolphin
is only two arm's lengths from me,
she rolls up from the water
and I can feel
the ripples of her path,
brushing over the creek
into my skin

like the sound waves of a symphony
washing through the audience.
I want to close my eyes,
drink it in,
but can't look away from her—
the glint of sunshine
on her skin, the lacy mist
of water as she breathes.
What are you doing here? I think.
Are you real?
As if in answer, the dolphin
turns her head
toward me
and rises, just a little bit,
from the water
so that I can see her wide smile
and then
she *spits* at me.
Just a little, the smallest spray
of cold water
splashing over my head.
Like she's saying,
Come on, silly, of course I'm real.
I'm so surprised
I can't react—
by the time I realize what happened

she's already moving on,
dancing down the river
like the most shocking thing
in my whole life
didn't just happen.

WHAT I KNOW ABOUT PENNY ROONEY, PART 3

Small girl, all bones
and points, with brown hair and eyes,

who can be brave
and do something secretly stupendous

and make a new friend
out of an entirely impossible thing.

TRUST

I pull on my clothes and creep inside, before
Mama sees my wet hair
and reminds me not to swim this week.
I corner Liana in her bedroom,
where she's working through her homework
for spring break, like the straight-A
student she's always been.
"Liana," I say.

Liana pauses. "Yeah, Cupcake?"

        I take a deep breath,
        letting the air fill my lungs
        from top to bottom,
        sink down to my toes,
        and rise out of the top of my head.

"I just saw the dolphin," I say
all in a rush. "I was on the dock
when it swam by."
I bite my lip.
"Don't tell Mama and Daddy,
but I jumped in, too. It swam right up to me.

It spit water at me
before it went away."

> I close my eyes,
> and I can see the dolphin's
> laughing smile
> like it's right in front of me again,
> the way her stream of water
> made her thoughts so clear.

"Whoa," Liana says. "Really?
Do you think it's still there?
Let's go see!"
We race outside.
"I wonder why it came back?"
Liana asks while we run across the lawn.
I breathe—
In through my nose,
Out through my mouth,
the way Daddy taught me to when I run.

The creek is empty
when we get there—

> no boats,
> no ducks,
> definitely no dolphins.

We watch for a long time,
but the only things we see
are the splashes of jumping fish
and a heron who glares beadily
from a floating log.

"You believe me, right?"
I ask, afraid if Liana doesn't see her,
my dolphin couldn't be real.
"Of course I do," Liana says.
"I know what I saw last week.
I just wish I could've been there.
Could've jumped in with her, too."

"Yeah," I say, and I wish that, too—
except for the small voice deep down inside
that whispers how nice it is
to have one thing Liana couldn't do
            that
        I
                    could.

TEXTING CRICKET

I text Cricket that night
while I do my breathing treatments.
                    You won't
                    believe this,
I write, my fingers hovering
over the screen a moment.
                    Guess what
                    I saw today?
                    A dolphin.
                    A dolphin
                    in OUR creek.
As I wait for her to reply,
my heart does that thing
where it feels like it's grown—
blood whooshing,
whooshing through my ears.
Will Cricket laugh at me?
Will she shoot back with
the scientific facts
and data I *know* says
what we saw isn't possible?
Before I can get too worked up,
the phone dings in my hand

and I look down to see
Cricket's written just one word:
COOL!!!
All that whooshing blood
goes back to normal in one
big, long, grateful sigh.
The phone dings again:
That's amazing!
Next time
call me
so I can see it too.
I don't mean to
but I can't help thinking
of how before long,
Cricket will be more than one backyard away.
If an impossible thing happens
two months from now,
she'll be all the way in Virginia.
The thought sends a twisty,
twirly feeling through my middle.
Thinking of Cricket in a whole other state
feels as lonely
as the dolphin must feel
miles and miles from her pod
in the blue-green sea.

TUESDAY MORNING

Tuesday morning, the dolphin comes—
and this time
I'm not the only one who sees.
I'm sitting on the dock,
feet swirling
in the water, thinking up a poem in my head.

Daddy's off work again—
most weeks he does three twelve-hour shifts,
which keep him gone till seven at night
but mean he only works three days.
Now he sits in a lawn chair,
fingers busy tying flies for fishing.
It's what he does
when he wants to relax,
because he says it's impossible
to pay attention to the fiddly little knots
and think about anything else.
Sometimes he uses the flies himself, or sells them
to the bait and tackle shop
a few minutes away.

Daddy's hands are big but agile,
good at little things

like tying flies or knitting, which he does
every winter, so that we all have handknit scarves
and pot holders—and once,
even a sweater that took him months
to make, which Mama says
makes her feel like she's wearing something
spun from gold.
Daddy says he learned to knit
in college,
when all those medical classes
got the better of him, and he started to feel
like his heart never stopped pounding.
Fly tying came later,
when he and Mama bought the house
on the water.

So we're sitting there, together-but-not
while the river spools by
and a bullfrog thrums, and a turtle
bobs its head up and back down,
when Daddy suddenly
sits straight up and says,

"Pen, did you see that over there?"
He's pointing
downstream, toward Cricket's house.
I watch for a moment

and then, sure enough, I see it:
the now-familiar dorsal
cutting through the water,
the shine of sun on gray rubber skin,
the smooth sleek back
gliding up and down.

I scramble to my feet. "That's it!" I cry. "That's her!"
And then I remember
I never told Daddy about the dolphin.
"I saw her yesterday," I babble, leaning out as far
over the water as I can,
straining my eyes to guess
where the water will part next.
"But Liana and me, we saw her Friday.
The day school ended.
Mama didn't believe us!
And when I Googled, I couldn't find anything
about dolphins in Turtle Creek—
but I knew it, Daddy. I knew what Liana and I saw."

Daddy and I watch
the dolphin swim lazily upstream,
and even though
there are more than ten feet
between us and the dolphin, in this moment
it feels like all three of us

are pulled together by a silver spiderweb
tying us into one heartbeat
the way Daddy ties all those fuzzy things
into his flies.
"It's beautiful," Daddy says, his voice quiet, reverent,
the way it gets when he says prayers
or catches sight of Mama looking especially pretty.
He rubs his eyes. "Who'd have thought?"
He pulls out his phone,
sends Mama a text:
COME OUTSIDE QUICK.

"Why would it come all this way?" I ask,
itching to dive in, to feel
water between me and my dolphin,
to see her wide smile—
but knowing if I asked, Daddy would say
no way, nohow.
"What's it doing so far from the sea?
Do you think it's in trouble?"

Daddy shrugs, says maybe the dolphin's hunting,
or that she could've lost her way.
In his voice, I can hear that he's torn
between wonder and worry, just like me.

SHARING THE IMPOSSIBLE

Mama makes it outside
right before the dolphin swims away—
Liana close behind,
so excited she's dancing.
Mama shields her eyes with her hand,
watches for a long skeptical moment, then—
gasps, as the dorsal
slices through the water one more time.
"Oh my goodness," she whispers.
"Oh my goodness.
Penny, y'all were right."
She holds her hand to her heart, like
she has to make sure
she's still alive,
make sure her heart's still beating,
make sure all this is real.

"Yes!" Liana whoops
and pumps an arm up in the air.
"I hoped it would come back."

"How many times you say y'all saw the dolphin?"
Daddy asks, his eyes narrowed thoughtfully.

"Only twice before," I say.
"Once yesterday. Once last week."

"How can we be sure it's the same dolphin?"
Mama asks,
a fair question.
I know in the wild, dolphin researchers sometimes
put on tracker tags,
or identify dolphins by their fins or something,
even though to me,
dolphin dorsals all look the same.

I can't say how I know
this is the same dolphin as before
except that the *knowing* tingles through me,
more certain than anything
I've ever known before, the same way
I know this dolphin is a she.
"It's her," I say. "I don't know how I know it,
but I do. I swear it's her."
The four of us watch the water, silent,
eyes fixed on the last place
we saw her fin break the river.
But the water's still as glass,
our dolphin gone downstream again.
My whole body feels like it's on fire

with the wish that I could've dived right in
and paddled along beside her.

Finally, Daddy says,
"Listen, girls, if y'all see her again,
you let me know, okay?
I've got a friend from college
who works at the Duke marine biology station.
She'd know what's going on here.
Know if something's wrong.
I think I'm gonna give her a call today."

But even the worry
that tickles at my stomach,
even Daddy's wrinkled forehead
and the whisper that maybe something's wrong
can't take away the deep, dazzling delight
of seeing my dolphin again.

"CERTAINLY UNUSUAL"

"I met Cecily in college," Daddy says
that afternoon as he dials his phone.
"Even back then, she only had eyes for the sea."

Dr. Cecily Zhao picks up after a few rings.
I sit and listen
to the one-sided conversation.
"Hi, Cecily," says Daddy.
A minute of small talk, and then
Daddy says, "Listen,
something unexpected happened here.
There's a dolphin in our creek—
we've seen it three times now.
Any guess what might be going on?
We're in Havelock, a mile
off the Neuse, on Turtle Creek.
It's maybe twenty-five yards wide."

He listens for a few minutes.
Finally, he says,
"Thanks, Cecily, I appreciate it.
I won't be here,
but Liz and the girls will.
I'll tell them to be on the lookout."

He hits the End Call button
and sets his phone down. "Cecily says
a dolphin this far upstream is certainly unusual.
Dolphins aren't uncommon
in the Neuse, especially farther east
where it empties into the Pamlico Sound.
Whole pods of dolphins
live in the Sound.
But they don't venture into little streams like ours.
This one may be a stray adventurer,
but Cecily would like to come
tomorrow while I'm at work and take a look,
see if she can find the dolphin
and figure out what's going on."

Can Dr. Cecily Zhao explain the way
the dolphin seemed to hear my thoughts?

Will she take the dolphin back
to her pod, so far away?

Can she tell me why
the dolphin feels already a part of my soul?

IN THE SMALL HOURS

Mama calls the time
when the clock starts over
after midnight

the small
hours
of the night.

I've always loved
those words,
the way they feel

quiet,
as still as the hours
themselves.

But I don't
love
being awake

for those
small hours
of the night.

Early, early Wednesday,
before any light
has touched the sky,

I come awake
all at once.
Cough, cough, cough.

The coughing
rattles through me,
stronger than sleep.

CF happens this way
sometimes—
creeps up on me

while I'm sleeping,
oozes
into my dreams,

like a secret,
silent
monster,

stealing the breath
right out
of my lungs.

THE OTHER SIDE OF THE COIN

Moments like this—
coughing and coughing
in the
      lonely
      dark
      hours
of the night,
unable to breathe without
feeling the deep-down
crackle pop buzz
of shifting mucus
tickling my airways—
moments like this
are when
I don't feel so much
like *one of the lucky ones*
after all.

MIDNIGHT MEDS

At first I try to go back to sleep,
but every time I lie down
the coughing starts again.
No matter which side I lie on
the coughing keeps on coming.

Finally, I wriggle out
of the covers,
let my feet fall onto the carpet,
drag my sleepy self
into the hallway.

In the darkness
Liana's there already,
in pajamas and bare feet.
Her dark brown hair
mussed and wild.
Her bedroom
is across the hall from mine.

"Pen," she says,
voice scratchy with sleep,
"I heard you coughing.
Want company?"

I nod.
Guilt slithers through me—
almost twelve is old enough
to do breathing treatments
without needing help.
And Liana isn't
my dad
or my mom.
She shouldn't have to lose sleep
because her baby sister
coughs too loud.

But wrapped up in the guilt
is a warm wave of relief
that I'm not alone.

Nothing is as lonely
as the middle of the night.

I follow Liana downstairs
and she helps me
load a nebulizer cup,
then plugs in the long air tube
and turns it on for me
while I put on my vest.

Most of the time,
I'd never let anyone else
do these things for me.
Daddy and Mama taught me
to handle all my treatments
years ago, and it feels weird
for anyone else to help.

But at two a.m.
all I know
about Penny Rooney
is that she is scared
and small.

When my machines
are rattling away,
Liana sits down on the couch by me
not caring about my shaking vest
and tucks us under
my purple rose blanket.
"Night-night, Bumblebee,"
she mumbles, and then
she falls asleep right there
snoring a little
(though she'd kill me
if I said she snores)
while my nebulizer mists the room.

PODLESS

Mama says some CF patients sleep
while they do treatments,
but I've never been able to.
Too much noise,
too many changes
in the vest vibration patterns,
too many medications that make my heart race.

So even though it's late, I stay awake.
I put a documentary about zoo vets on TV,
quiet for Liana's sake,
but can't focus.
Instead, I think about the dolphin—

how she's all alone out there,
no sun-sparkled family to surround her,
nobody who understands
exactly what she's going through.
Here on the couch, even
with Liana sleeping beside me—

I think I understand
how that podless dolphin feels.

THE SIX-FOOT RULE

I know more
than most people about germs
and how
they travel. For as long
as I remember,
I've known about
the six-foot rule—
the way you have to stay
six feet apart
from other CF patients.

CF worms its way
into almost every organ, but
its *favorite*
playground is your lungs.
It fills them
up with sticky, gooey mucus,
invites bacteria
to move on in, glues together
delicate airways
so you can't catch your breath.

        Every CF patient
has their own colony of germs
            living in
their clogged-up lungs—
            bacteria
that come from soil, water,
            even air.
Those germs don't make
            healthy people
sick, but can be deadly
            for CF lungs.
My lungs can't pass my germs
            to yours—
unless you have CF.

        So it's a rule:
if two CF patients meet,
            we have to stay
six feet apart, wearing masks
            so our bacteria
can't decide to travel into
            someone else's lungs.
It's a rule nobody ever knows
            unless they have CF,
the kind of thing that blows
            most people's minds

when I explain it—how I've
        never had a CF camp
or even a hospital support group,
        never hugged
another person like me.

        For me
it's part of every day,
        that six-foot rule.
I see other CF patients
        sometimes,
at the clinic or the hospital.
        I can always tell
them by their masks, their
        poky bones,
the way they're short, like me.
        We wave sometimes
across a great big room,
        me and those
familiar strangers,
        but we don't
get close, don't high-five or hug,
        or sit shoulder-
to-shoulder and talk about
        nebulizers

or
how lonely
night
can
be.

WHEN THE MORNING COMES

I wake up
only a few hours
after midnight meds

and notice
two things
right away:

First, a tickle
in my throat
and cotton in my head

that weren't there
last night. And second,
that what woke me

was not a sound
or a touch
or even a dream—

it was something
deep inside me,
a wordless call

that still rings
in my head
like the echo

of a shout, bouncing
off the walls
of a canyon.

It's barely six thirty
according to
my bedside clock,

but I'm already
wide awake
and standing up

before I even
really realize
what I'm doing.

Daddy's gone
to work already,
but nobody else stirs.

Liana and I
both went back to bed
after my treatment finished.

The sun
is barely up;
the whole world

bathed in the dim
gray light
of early morning.

I walk on silent
feet downstairs,
slip through the door,

and step
out onto
dew-wet grass.

When I've finished
running through
the half-lit backyard,

my feet hit
the rough
splintered dock

and she is there
exactly where I knew
she'd be:

my dolphin,
silver, grinning.
Waiting for me.

SECRET SWIM

I don't even have to think this time:
I pull off my fuzzy pj pants
and glasses
and dive right in,
the cold-
water shock
zipping through my senses
like those Pop Rocks candies
that explode the moment you put them
on your tongue.
In this moment, all else
is forgotten—the tickle
in my throat,
the exhaustion
of my late-night breathing treatments.
I'm not thinking of anything
except the water
closing over my head—
and then, as I come up for air,
the dolphin in the creek
right in front of me,
her permanent smile, her wise bright eyes,
the way she dips her head down

and up to splash me, just like
she did on Monday.

I tread water, legs and arms
spinning, and watch
as she swims a slow circle
around me. I can feel her wake,
tiny waves that ripple against my skin.
When she's done, she rolls
her whole body over,
like a dog that wants to play.
I'm afraid even to breathe, in case
I might wake up from this dream
between one breath and the next.
Slowly, carefully, I reach
my hand out, the way I might
with Cricket's skittish cat.
I let my hand float there.
And then—and then—
the dolphin glides forward in the water,
bops my hand ever-so-gently
with the end of her snout, and swims away.
Like a little kid
playing *tag, you're it*.
For a minute I think she's gone
but then she's back, swimming

another circle around me, splashing
cold creek water into my face,
smiling that cheerful smile.
And I know she can't understand my words,
but I whisper them anyway:
"How did I know you'd be here
this morning?"
How could that knowing have pulled me
from my sleep, brought me outside,
at the exact moment she was here?

The dolphin doesn't answer,
just bats my hand again
and then, with one final playful roll,
she's gone, swimming away
into the golden morning light.

DR. CECILY ZHAO

I call Cricket Wednesday afternoon
before Dr. Cecily Zhao comes.
"Come over here," I say,
"so you can meet the dolphin doctor."
Cricket shouts to her mom
to ask permission, and then says,
"I can come, as long as I'm back
this evening, to help with packing."

Mama makes me do an extra treatment first—
the cough that started last night
still lingers in my lungs,
heavy and thick.
"Hopefully just allergies,"
Mama says,
a pinch between her eyebrows.

We all wait out front:
me, Cricket, Mama, Liana.
Cricket's practically jumping up and down,
her pale face shining
at the chance to meet a real live scientist.
Liana's trying to stay calm,

but I can see the little wiggle in her hips.
Liana's feelings *always* come out
through singing or through dance.
Mama keeps checking the time
nervously on her phone.

By the time Dr. Cecily Zhao pulls up
in our driveway,
I'm not sure
if my hands shake more
from the albuterol neb I did beforehand
or the anticipation.

Dr. Zhao is petite, like me,
but somehow her shoulders-back, head-up
way of walking
says, *Step aside,*
the doctor is in the house.
Two college interns trail behind her—
a tall bronze-skinned boy
and a sunburned blond girl.

"Lovely to meet you, Elizabeth,"
Dr. Zhao says,
shaking Mama's hand.
"Please, call me Cecily.

These are my interns,
Esteban and Madison."

They follow us around back
to the dock, set down their mysterious
equipment bags, unzip.
"We'll take samples of the river here.
We'll measure the salinity,
check for pathogens or chemicals.
With any luck, your dolphin friend
will swim along while we work."

Mama nods. "Girls—
don't interrupt Dr. Zhao, all right?
Cecily, please,
let me know if there's anything you need."
Mama goes back inside,
but me and Cricket and Liana stay,
watching the scientists
like they're magicians.

AT THE LAST MOMENT

Dr. Zhao and her interns stay a long time.
Long enough for us
to get bored
and retreat to the patio
to play a game of Nerts.

The scientists take water samples,
talk in voices that carry
through the clear spring air.
Sometimes they laugh, or go silent,
bent over calculations.
Finally, they zip their tools
back into their bags. I can tell
by the slump of Madison's shoulders,
by Esteban's half-hearted shrug,
that the dolphin didn't show.
They pick up their bags
and start to walk our way.

I forget to watch the game
and Liana slaps her last card down
with a "Ha!" of triumph.
Cricket groans, but I hardly notice.
I wish Dr. Zhao had seen the dolphin.

I wish so hard, it's like
a spark inside me
reaching right down to my toes.

And at that moment,
right there at the glass-topped table on our deck
where Cricket and Liana count their scores—

I feel it.

    A zinging,
      singing kind of thing
           that pours through me
           like summer rain.

She's here.

I drop my cards,
surge up from the chair,
shout,
"Wait! Don't go!"
I run toward the dock,
grass tickling my bare feet.
"I think I see it," I call, even though it's a lie.
"I think she's here! The dolphin!
Come on!"

I sail by the scientists.
My feet hit the warm old dock wood
and right away I see her,
that now-familiar silver fin.
"Look!" I say.

For a minute, they are quiet, and then
Madison gasps.
"I see it!" she cries, full of wonder.
Cricket and Liana run up
and I can feel them standing
at my shoulders, like an extension
of my own body.
Cricket squeals softly.

"Oh wow," says Dr. Zhao.
The dolphin,
my dolphin,
is turning, turning in the water,
swimming right

      up

           to

                  our

                        dock.

UP CLOSE,
IN LIVING COLOR

The dolphin is
the most beautiful
thing my eyes

have ever seen.
So close.
She lifts her

shining head
just enough,
showing us

her beaming smile,
her night-black,
world-wise liquid eyes.

She is so close,
so clear,
so real—

the realest thing
I think that I
have ever seen.

I kneel down
on the dock
and rest my hand

in the water.
She does not
come closer,

but she doesn't
move away,
either.

I breathe,
and breathe,
and breathe,

and think maybe
I have never
breathed so deep.

"Wow,"
says Dr. Zhao
again, her voice

as reverent
as Mama's is
when she prays.

"Esteban,
are you getting
this on film?

Penny, you must
have excellent
vision, to have seen

this from all
the way up
on the deck."

I can't explain
to Dr. Zhao
that it wasn't

anything
to do with *seeing*,
only *knowing*.

But how
could I
have known?

DOLPHIN WATCHING

"Penny, could you move a bit?"
Dr. Zhao asks.
It's almost painful to take my hand
out of the water,
shake the wetness off,
stand up, step back onto the grass,
so Dr. Zhao and her interns
can take my place.

The scientists perch
on the dock.
Dr. Zhao asks Madison
to make notes about the time,
the date, how warm the water is,
everything
they might need to know.

Esteban hands Dr. Zhao
a blue cooler.
It's full of ice and dead fish,
smelling like the one Daddy uses
when he goes fishing
with the flies he ties.

I plug my nose. Gross.
Dr. Zhao tosses a cold, dead fish
to the dolphin.
The dolphin doesn't catch it—she sinks
her head back under the water,
leaving just a ripple.

Dr. Zhao waits patiently
like it doesn't matter
that the dolphin spurned her gift.
Soon enough
I see the glint of sun on rubber skin.
The dolphin raises her head
so that her thoughtful eye meets Dr. Zhao's.
"The round part of her head
is called the melon," Dr. Zhao says.
"She uses it to echolocate—
it's how she 'sees' in water."
The dolphin sinks under again
then rises out, like a kid
playing hide-and-seek.
When Dr. Zhao throws another fish,
the dolphin scoops it up.
"Dolphins are curious,"
says Dr. Zhao. "Sometimes, it's enough
if you give them something

to be curious about.
From the size, I'm guessing
she's an adult female."

The dolphin lingers for a moment
after her fishy snack,
looking from side to side,
sizing those scientists up.
When she sinks a final time
I can see her sleek shadow underneath
the dark of Turtle Creek—

turning,
      swimming
away
      upstream.

CELEBRATION

Cricket bounces with excitement.
"I can't believe it!" she whispers,
waving her arms like wings,
like fins.
Liana grabs Cricket's hands
and twirls her along the grass.
I don't say anything at all.

> My heart
> too full
> of dolphin.

WHAT COMES NEXT

Dr. Zhao stands
and Purells her stinky, fishy hands.
"Thanks, Penny," she says.
"You might have the makings
of a dolphin whisperer."
She smiles, like a joke—
but I know what just happened
feels like *magic* more than science.

"What comes next?" I ask.

"We'll take the samples to the lab,"
she says, "and run some tests.
We'll come back with a bigger team
and give the dolphin a full exam.
She looks okay but seems a little lethargic—
that means she's swimming slower
than she might.
Creeks like this aren't good for her,
and we want to make sure she isn't sick.
Then, after that—well, we'll see."

Dr. Zhao digs in her pocket,
pulls out a crisp white business card.
"Your daddy said you were the first to see
the dolphin, right?" she asks.
"I can tell you really love her."
I nod, not knowing how to put into words
the way it feels when the dolphin
rolls out of the water,
sparkling in the springtime sun.
"You let me know
when you see her again,"
Dr. Zhao goes on.
"Send me an email or a text
if she pops up in your creek.
I'll let your parents know
when we'll be back."

With a little wave, Dr. Zhao
and Madison and Esteban are gone.

A DOLPHIN NAMED ROSE

"We should name her,"
Cricket says.
"Well. One of *you* should.
You discovered her."
She looks at Liana and me.

Liana shrugs.
"I dunno," she says.
"Dolly Dolphin?"
She laughs
when Cricket and I
wrinkle up our noses.

I think of the dolphin's
ever-smile,
the way she splashes me,
how sliding
into the water beside her
taught me
that Penny Rooney
can be brave.

I think of the spring
world bursting into life
and the purple rose blanket
Liana spread over us
last night in the small hours.

"Rose," I say.
A name as beautiful
as silver dolphin skin
and as sad
as a creature lost
from her beloved pod.

"Rose," Cricket says.
"Rose," repeats Liana.
"I like it.
It's a good name, Rose."

And when Liana says that,
I can *feel* the dolphin—
Rose—
somewhere in the creek,
her great big heart
beating in time with mine.

GOING VIRAL

When I wake up Thursday morning
my cough is deep
and thick, full of gross green mucus
that I spit into tissue after tissue.
But even through the fog
of whatever is going on,
I can feel her the moment
I wake up—Rose, calling me,
calling from the creek.
Daddy's gone to work again
and Liana always sleeps late
on no-school days.
Mama's clicking away
on her laptop at the table
and doesn't look up
when I slip out the back door.

It's a warm yellow morning
bathed in sun, and my lungs
breathe just a little easier
here in the wide wonder of the world.
Rose is in the creek—
just like I knew she'd be.

Rose bats at my hand, like a dog
that wants to play, then ducks under,
and when she comes up,
sprays me—
not a funny little spit like the other day
but a LOT this time,
drenching my pajamas to the skin.
There won't be a way
to hide this from Mama.
And in one wild, foolish moment,
I ignore the pressure in my head
and the crackles in my lungs
and any sense I've ever had, and
rip my glasses off and

        jump

             right

                  in.

Rose makes room as I jump, but then
she's right beside me, her body so much bigger
when I'm this close
that it takes my breath away.
But she's gentle, so gentle,
as she nudges me with her smiling snout.
I can almost *hear* Rose in my head
begging me to play.

I splash her and she splashes back,
drenching any part of me
that wasn't wet already.
Then she nudges me and zips across the creek
like she wants me to follow.
I tuck into a freestyle stroke, pulling
at the water, trying to keep my breathing even
and ignore the sloshy wetness in my lungs,
trying to hold the coughs in
even though Dr. Theo always tells me not to.

Rose is waiting for me at the other side
and she takes off again, downstream this time,
rolling in the water so her white belly
flashes in the morning sun.
But I'm wearing out now, the heaviness
in my body catching up to me.
I tread water while I cough, cough, cough,
feeling like the whole creek is *inside* me.
After a minute, Rose circles back
and nudges me again, like she's asking
why I didn't come.

"Sorry, Rose," I say, and rub
a cautious hand across her head. "I can't."
Rose nudges me, gentler this time,

makes a strange crooning noise.
She swims a circle around me, slow and careful,
then butts up against my side.

"Hey," I say. "Stop that."
But she does it again—a gentle push,
rubbing her silken body against mine, and when
I raise my hand to pat her again,
she glides forward so that I catch
her dorsal, not her head.
Her fin is tall and strong, firmer than the rest of her,
slick wet stone against my fingers.
She swims around me again
and then does the exact same thing,
pushing up against me, and this time

I close my eyes
and take a breath
and let my fingers curl around her fin—

and with one kick of her powerful tail
we are gliding through the water,
Rose pulling me along,
clicking joyfully as we go.

SWIMMING WITH ROSE

Is like flying
like skating
like dreaming
like dancing.

CONNECTION

Rose pulls me upstream
then oh so gently
turns a half circle
and takes me back.
I can feel
the muscles
under her smooth skin,
so much power and strength
it makes me dizzy,
almost scared,
except that it's impossible
to be scared
with my fingers on her fin,
like somehow
the nerves in my fingertips
are receiving signals
right from the dolphin's heart
and what they say is
love,
love,
love.

I don't know
if Rose is telling me
her thoughts
or if I'm making it all up,
but what I know is
I have never felt anything
at all like this before.

MAMA

I'm so swept up
in my dream-true
dolphin moment,

so full of a feeling
I can't possibly name,
that it isn't until Rose

stills in the water,
goes wary,
shrugs off my hand,

that I look up

    and
    see
  Mama.

A BAD IDEA

"Penny!"
Mama's jaw works
like she's trying to say more,
but no words come.
"Penny Elizabeth Rooney,
what are you doing?"
she chokes out at last.
Beside me, Rose pulls away,
sinks down
under the water
so only half her great, liquid eye
is visible. She doesn't stay—
just lingers for one breath
then disappears
into the creek
and, with a few strong strokes,
is gone.

I want to race after her,
hold forever to the magic
of this morning in the water—
but it's just me now,
and the chill

seeping into my skin.
I clench my teeth
so they won't chatter.
I remember now that I am sick,
that the creek is inside me
as well as out,
that everything I've just done
is a very, very bad idea.

I swim to the dock
with heavy arms.
Water streams from my pajamas
when I climb out,
and I try hard not to shiver
while Mama watches.
She stares at me a long time,
dripping on the boards below us,
and then she sadly shakes her head
and turns to go inside,
her silence so much worse
than any scolding she might give.

WHAT I HAVE IN ME

When we get inside
Mama takes my sodden pajamas
and throws them in the wash
as I start the shower.
When I'm dressed again
Liana's awake,
humming in her bedroom
across the hall.
She pokes her head out.
"Did I just see you
in soaking-wet pajamas?"
Her bedroom window
faces the backyard.

I nod and bite my lip,
remembering Monday, how Liana
wished she could have been there
in the water with Rose.
I love my sister, but I'm still not sad
to have one thing
that's mine alone.
"I knew you had it in you,
Petit Chou," Liana says.

I stick out my tongue when she calls me
little cabbage.

I don't know how Liana
could have known
that somewhere deep within me
there exists a Penny who is brave,
bold, breaking all the rules—
because until this week
I had no idea
I held any of this inside.

AN EXPLANATION

When I get downstairs
Mama's at the kitchen table,
a cup of tea that smells
like dead things
steaming beside her.
"Echinacea," she says,
pushing the mug toward me.
"Good for colds.
Now talk."

"I didn't plan to do it,"
I say, and mean it,
even though
I keep *not planning*
to swim with Rose
and it keeps
happening anyway.
"I just wanted
to see her, Mama."

Mama's eyebrow curls,
a skeptical expression
that makes me want to shiver—
from guilt this time.

"All right," she says,
and there is danger
lurking in the calm
reasonableness
of her voice.
"You didn't plan it.
How exactly, then,
did you end up
in the water
with a
*four-hundred-pound
wild animal?*"

I look into the murky depths
of my echinacea tea.
"She comes in the morning,"
I say at last.
"Yesterday
I woke up early, and she
was at the dock."

Mama presses her lips
in a terrible thin line
and doesn't speak.

"So I thought I'd see
if she was there today.

I petted her,
and she splashed me,
and I figured
since I was already wet . . ."
Mama doesn't answer
so I dig myself in deeper.
"We were playing.
She isn't dangerous, Mama.
She's so *gentle*.
It sounds weird,
but I told her I felt sick
and couldn't swim, and she—
she *told* me
to take her fin
and then she pulled me
through the river."

"She told you,"
says Mama flatly.

A blush creeps up
my face, and I sneeze—
like even my cold is a tiny bit
embarrassed for me.
"I know how it sounds,
but it's true.

I don't know
how she told me.
But she made me know
exactly what she thought."

"What she thought,"
says Mama,
"is neither here nor there.
I'd like to know exactly what
my *daughter* thought
that made her decide
to sneak out
to go swimming
in a creek in April when she's
                    already
                         sick!"

I look down.
Sip my tea—
even the honey swirled through
isn't enough to fix the taste.
Like black licorice
and mushroom and mold,
like licking the forest floor.
"I'm sorry," I say at last.
"It was dumb."

I mean what I say, but still—
I can't shake that
marvelous spectacular
stupendous feeling
as Rose pulled me through the water,
that *love, love, love*
that pulsed
from her heart to mine.

"It was," says Mama.
"Penny, I expected
better. This isn't like you,
sneaking and lying
and making choices
that put your health in jeopardy.
You're more mature than this."

Adults have always said
I'm so *mature*
when what they mean is
I don't complain about my treatments.

"I'm going to call Dr. Theo
to see what she says about this cold."
Mama's voice
is frayed and tired,

every word slanting up
like she's questioning
everything she's ever known
about her daughter.

And maybe I am, too.

Mama stands.
"And maybe after that,
you should send a text
to Dr. Zhao
to let her know
that Rose was here."

CALLING DR. THEO

Dr. Theo
is my CF doctor,
all the way in Durham.

She has a Boston accent
a kind smile
and a brilliant mind.

An hour after her phone call
Mama says
she's going to the pharmacy—

Dr. Theo called in
some antibiotics
just in case.

SILENT WARNINGS

When you have cystic fibrosis
   just in case
thrums through your veins
   like a drumbeat,
a silent, sinister reminder
   of how bad
things could really get.

"Hopefully the meds
   will kick in
before Monday morning,"
   Mama says,
and her voice holds the ghost
   of future *maybe*s.
If I'm not better by Monday,
   what about school?
What about bus rides
   with Cricket
in the six weeks we have left?
   What about
Ms. Berman's poetry slam?
   What if
the judges choose my poem

> but I stay sick
so I'm not there to read it?

Last time things got really bad
> in fourth grade,
I missed weeks and weeks,
> had to turn in
all my work on Google Classroom.
> I even missed
the end-of-fourth-grade party.
> Mama took a picture:
me on the couch, pale and sick,
> just days
out of the hospital, watching
> my class
celebrate . . . on Zoom.

If I'm not better by Monday
> how many
days or weeks or months
> could CF
decide to steal from me?

CRICKET'S HOUSE

I go to Cricket's Thursday afternoon.
Mama says she's pretty sure
I'm not *sick* sick, just *CF* sick,
which can't hurt anyone but me
or someone else with roses in their DNA.
We lie on Cricket's bed
and talk about Dr. Zhao and Rose
and about school
and Lyla Rain,
the girl who sits behind me in homeroom
who Cricket has a crush on.
I don't tell her
about my *just in case* antibiotics
or how Mama said *hopefully*
I'll be better Monday—like it was a question.

"Are you going to submit a poem
to the sixth-grade poetry slam?" I ask.
Cricket nods.
"Yeah, probably," she says.
"I'm thinking maybe something
about the time in first grade
when Mom took me to Florida

to see the rocket launch.
That's when I *knew* for sure that someday
I wanted to be the person
helping get those rockets off the ground."

I look up at the ceiling
of Cricket's bedroom, covered
with glow-in-the-dark galaxies—
it's even got
a papier-mâché model
of the planets in our solar system,
all spaced around her ceiling light,
as if it were the sun.
This whole room is Cricket, wall to wall:
a giant blueprint of Apollo 11,
the rocket that first took men to the moon;
her comforter is chalkboard green,
patterned with equations
I couldn't begin to understand.

It's different from my bedroom
with its blue-gray walls,
a yellow daisy comforter,
a few pictures here and there:
a bunch of kids with white-robed Jesus,
a framed print of *Starry Night*,

a family picture from when I was eight.
I love my room,
but it wouldn't teach you much
about Penny Rooney.

"What about you?" asks Cricket.
"You're submitting a poem, right?"
Cricket's one of the only people on earth
who's seen some of my poems.
"What's it going to be about?
They'll pick you for the slam for sure!"
I shrug, hearing the whispery buzz
when I breathe in
that means my lungs are full of junk.
"I don't know yet," I say.
"I can't figure out what to write.
It's weird, isn't it?
Shouldn't I know more than anyone
about myself?"
I cough into my elbow.

"You could write about CF," Cricket says,
"or . . ." She stops and bites her lip.
"Maybe about the dolphin.
Or singing. Those duets with Liana!"
But I'm not so sure.

CF isn't all there is to me,
and Rose is *her* own self, not mine.
Singing is Liana's special thing—
something she shares with me,
not something of my own.
"I'll figure it out," I say,
and we're quiet for a moment, until Cricket
speaks up with a tiny crack
in her voice.

"Mama's already scheduled the truck,"
Cricket says, kicking her foot
at a cardboard box beside the bed.
"The *moving* truck. To take all our stuff
up to Virginia.
It's coming June 11th. Two days
after school is done."
We both look at the NASA calendar
hanging on Cricket's wall.
April's already almost over.
May will feel shorter than a blink.
How is our time running out so fast?
I cough again.
"Are you feeling okay?" asks Cricket,
forehead wrinkling.

"I'm fine," I say, waving my hand
as if I could brush it all away.
I try to buckle in my coughs,
so they can't tear a hole
in the words that build a bridge between us,
tying us together
even though we're surrounded on all sides
by cardboard boxes, flaps spread wide,
waiting, waiting,
to pack up Cricket's life.

THE NEXT DAY

I

am

worse.

EXASPERATION

When you get *CF* sick—
sick
from those bacteria
that love your lungs
so much—
it is called
a *CF exacerbation.*

> Exacerbate:
> "to make
> a problem
> worse."

A normal person
would call it *pneumonia,*
but it's different with CF.
Up until age ten
I couldn't remember
the right word
so I said
CF exasperation.

Exasperate:
"to make someone
very angry
or annoyed."

To be honest,
I think maybe
I was right
all along.

EXTRA, EXTRA

Mama calls Dr. Theo again,
who orders me to up my treatments.
Mama glues on a smile, says,
"At least it's been a while, right?"

She isn't wrong—
my lungs have been clean and clear
a whole year without antibiotics
so that I almost forgot
what it felt like
when they're filled up with goo.
It's been kind of like a miracle, this year.

But no matter how long it's been
since the last exacerbation
it always feels too soon.

I do treatments every four hours,
vest shaking
nebulizer misting
as I switch between dolphin documentaries
and the poetry slam contest.
What do I know about Penny Rooney,
really?

At this point
I don't even know
if Penny Rooney will be back at school
when it starts up again
in just three days.

ROSE

Dr. Zhao calls after lunch,
says she and her team
will head out soon
on a boat this time
to give Rose a medical exam.
I wander outside to wait—
        no Cricket today,
        since her mama
        has her sorting:
        things to take,
        things to toss.
The creek is quiet, sun hot
on my shoulders.
I go right to the dock.
The wood is rough
but familiar,
like when I step onto it
I can feel every sun-washed day
of childhood, every moment I spent
swimming or fishing or just laying out.
Now, I stretch myself
on my stomach,
prop my chin in my arms

on the edge of the dock, so that the water
is only a breath away.

I close my eyes and silently call.
>	*Rose.*
>	*Rose.*
>	*Come.*

I don't know how to describe, exactly,
the way I reach inside myself
and find some thread of me
that is connected to her,
but I do. And after only a few minutes
of lying there on the sun-warmed dock,
I see her, cutting through the water.

Already, she feels like a familiar friend.

FRIEND

She swims right up to me today,
gives me the gentlest of splashes,
then brings her melon head right up
to my outstretched hand,
lets me rub her rubber skin while she
squeaks and clicks.

How did you know to come?
I think. Maybe I never woke up
this morning at all,
and this whole thing
is a part of some amazing dream.
How did you hear my call?

Rose bats playfully at my hand.
In one of those dolphin documentaries
I learned that dolphins shed old skin
every two hours—
that's what keeps their silver epidermis
so smooth and sleek.

Lying on my stomach like this
makes all the goop in my lungs shift

and slide,
and I have to take my hand
away from Rose to cough
and cough
and cough some more.
Rose doesn't move—she stays perfectly
beautifully still
there in the water, and even though
we're not touching anymore,
it feels like she's holding me
through every single cough.

I wish she and I could really talk.
I'd say *CF sucks sometimes,*
and somehow I know she'd understand.
She'd tell me what it feels like
to be stuck in Turtle Creek
when your home is miles and miles away.
And maybe Rose, with her amazing lungs
that can hold in air for ten whole minutes,
could teach me something
about what it really means to breathe.

DR. ZHAO RETURNS

I can hear the boat before I see it,
the engine puttering to a stop

when the scientists
are in view.

Rose sinks warily under
the surface, water rippling in her wake.

Dr. Zhao waves. I wave back.
She has Esteban and Madison again,

but also a bunch of other people,
some in the boat with Dr. Zhao,

others motoring behind them
in a Zodiac—

an air-inflated rubber boat
that putt-putts low across the water.

"Wow!" Dr. Zhao calls over.
"I see you've got our patient all ready.

We'll wait a minute before we come
too close, let her adjust."

At first I think Rose is gone,
but then I see a glint of silver

deep under the water,
lurking in the murky mud.

Slowly, so slowly
Dr. Zhao nudges forward,

a little at a time,
motor hardly sputtering

but it's not until she cuts it out
and waves at the Zodiac driver

to turn his motor off too
that the shining head returns.

A DOLPHIN AT THE DOCTOR

Rose doesn't get too close
to the boats, though I can tell
she's interested
from the way she pops up from the water
and then glides back down,
like a game of peekaboo.

Dr. Zhao directs her team
like an orchestra conductor.
> *Get the buoys there. Okay, you four,*
> *slide the net gently into the water.*
> *Esteban, will you prep some syringes? Thanks.*
They move like dancers,
all those scientists.
Within minutes, they've got a floating net
in the water, the Zodiac pulled close.
Some of the people are in the river,
others in the Zodiac. Still others
float on skinny rafts.
Dr. Zhao makes clucking, chuckling noises
in Rose's direction, tosses her a fish
from the same cooler she brought Wednesday.
Rose catches it this time—

like even with all the extra people,
she remembers Dr. Zhao, and trusts her.

"She's unusually calm," Dr. Zhao says,
her voice carrying clearly to the dock,
even through the surgical mask
she's pulled over her nose and mouth—
just like a human doctor.
"Still a bit lethargic. That can be a sign
of stress or illness."

       Slowly,
          s l o w l y,
Dr. Zhao coaxes Rose forward
until Rose is in the net, and all the people
pull it taut, so she can't swim away.
Rose thrashes a little—nervous, maybe,
surprised at Dr. Zhao's fishy betrayal.
I feel a pang, somewhere deep inside my own chest.
It's okay, it's okay, I think with all my might.

       In the water,
       Rose stills.

Dr. Zhao's team leaps into action:
one person looks at her wide, wise eyes;

another slides a needle into her tail fin;
somebody else fixes a plastic tracker to her dorsal;
yet another places a container
over Rose's blowhole as she exhales
what looks like—*ew*—
dolphin snot.
Dr. Zhao herself pulls out a stethoscope,
just like Dr. Theo at all my CF visits.
Esteban the intern is in charge
of plying Rose with fish.
He speaks to her in a low voice,
and surprisingly, she tolerates it all—though
I can tell from the way her tail swishes
through the water,
her patience won't last forever.

> *Good girl*, I think, *good girl*,
> and Rose meets my eye
> through that mess of people,
> and her enormous body quiets.

In a matter of minutes, the exam is done.
Scientists pack stethoscopes and needles.
Some climb into the Zodiac
while others swim back to the big boat.
The sides of the net are lowered—

and Rose is free.
She wriggles and writhes her way out
until she's back in the open river,
and with a final scolding snort in our direction,
she disappears below the water.

DIAGNOSIS

          Mama and Liana
make their way outside by the time
          the Zodiac has roared to life
and carried half the team away downstream.
          Finally, only Dr. Zhao, her interns,
and a few other people are left.
          Dr. Zhao drives the boat
right next to the dock, leaps off
          in one graceful jump.
"The news is good and bad," she says.
          "Her vitals are strong.
She's not in immediate distress.
          The bad news is:
I think she has pneumonia. I heard
          decreased breath sounds,
and there was bloody discharge in her sputum."
          (I already know from my CF life
that *sputum* is medical for *mucus*.)
          Dr. Zhao looks tired.
"This diagnosis is consistent with
          a stranded dolphin;
it's likely that she inhaled something
          in the dirty, brackish water

that made her sick. It could be the reason
  she hasn't made it back to her pod.
It would also explain the lethargy I noticed."

Pneumonia. Not so different
from the CF exacerbation blazing its way
  through my lungs right now.
The word tingles through my chest,
  makes my heart beat fast.
Dolphins are mammals, with lungs
  and breath like us,
but I'd never thought that maybe
  Rose could be
the exact same kind of sick as me.

  "What will you do next?"
Mama asks. "Can you treat pneumonia
  in a wild dolphin?"
Dr. Zhao sighs. "We can, and will,
  once we get the results
of that sputum culture and know what drugs
  we ought to try.
But regardless of the exact bacteria she's got,
  this dolphin needs to be back home.
That's a harder problem to solve, when a creature's
  stranded so far from high salinity.

For now, we'll figure out what bacteria
     we're dealing with,
then use the tracker we placed to find her
     and give her antibiotics.
Hopefully when she's feeling better,
     she'll be ready for a longer swim.
Hopefully when she's feeling better,
     she'll return back home.
By Monday, we'll have some answers.
     By Monday, we'll know what to do."

     "And what if she doesn't go back?"
I ask, my voice all rough thanks to
     my scratchy, painful throat.
"What if Rose doesn't want to leave Turtle Creek?"
     Dr. Zhao's eyebrows pull together.
"Rose?" she asks. I blush. Heat spreads
     across my cheeks.
"I named her Rose. I mean, that's just what we call her."
     Dr. Zhao smiles. "I like that," she says.
"Rose. Madison, make a note of that name.
     As for what will happen
if she decides to stick around—we'll have to cross
     that bridge later on.
I hope that when she's better, we won't have to.
     For now, just keep an eye out, Penny.

Feel free to text or email me anytime
　　　　you see Rose in your creek, okay?"

"Okay," I say, and though
I know Dr. Zhao is probably just being nice
　　　　because I'm a kid,
it still feels like I'm a real part of her team.
　　　　With a quick wave
at me and Mama and Liana, Dr. Zhao leaps
　　　　back onto her boat.
The motor grumbles awake, and they skim away
　　　　back downstream.

SATURDAY MORNING

I don't sleep in
and I don't wake up
because of Rose.

        I wake coughing,
        chest shaking
        throat aching
        skin burning.

I stumble out of bed
and down the stairs
and curl up in my therapy chair
with a nebulizer clutched in my teeth.

THE LAST DAYS OF SPRING BREAK

Drag on and on
a mess of nebs
and meds
and texts with Cricket.
A million milliseconds
of Mama
trying to pretend
she isn't worried.
I don't see Rose, don't feel
anything inside myself
except the crackle-pop
of infection.

"Listen to her?"
Mama asks Daddy
when he gets home
Saturday night.
Daddy rubs his stethoscope
to warm it,
puts it against my chest.
"Some rattling,
but not too bad," he says
with his serious-

respiratory-therapist face.
"I don't think we need
to call Dr. Theo just yet."

"Can I go over to Cricket's
and help her pack?" I ask
on Sunday afternoon,
and Mama says
not this time—
I need to rest and do more nebs.
Cricket texts a photo
of the bookshelves
in her living room, all the books
gone, packed
into moving boxes.
      I really wish
      you were feeling better,
she texts,
and I write back
      me too
even though those two words
don't even come close
to how I actually feel.
My insides are a tangled mess
of feelings I'm not brave
enough to look at yet.

QUESTIONS I DON'T ASK

I don't have to ask
to know
I'm not going
back to school
on Monday.

I've only got six weeks
with my BFF before she moves
hours away
and here I am, stuck at home,
wasting
       day
            after
                 day.

(Not) Back to school

DR. ZHAO'S PLAN

Daddy's phone rings
first thing Monday.
It's just him and me,
with Mama and Liana
back to school.
Daddy has Mondays off—
      so he's stuck with me,
      stuck at home.

Daddy turns on speakerphone
while Dr. Zhao explains
her plans for Rose.
"I hoped she'd find her way
back to the sea by now,
but the tracker says she hasn't.
Rose's sputum culture
was positive for the bacteria
Pseudomonas aeruginosa—"

"I know what that is!"
I shout, then pause to

COUGH,
     COUGH,
          COUGH.

"I have that, too!" I croak
when all the coughing's done.
Pseudomonas bacteria
is found all around us
in soil and water
and it *loves* CF lungs.
The antibiotics Dr. Theo prescribed,
the nebulizer mist
I breathe in every day—
both treat *Pseudo a.*

       One more thread linking
       Rose and me.

Dr. Zhao goes on:
"Today, we'll use the tracker
to find Rose and give her antibiotics.
Then we'll monitor her awhile.
As long as that goes okay,
if she's still in Turtle Creek
we'll send a full team up there

to try to lure her to the Neuse.
We want to get her
back to the Pamlico Sound—
we think that's where her pod lives."

RESEARCHING

After we hang up
with Dr. Zhao
I open the computer
and type
dolphin pneumonia
into the search bar—
then backspace,
replace it with
dolphin Pseudomonas.
A bunch
of doctor-ese articles
pop up
that I don't really
understand,
but I read enough
to know
that Dr. Zhao is right—
Pseudomonas aeruginosa
(and even other
CF bacteria
I've heard of
but don't have,
like

Mycobacterium abscessus)
can make dolphins sick,
just like me.

Maybe Rose and I
are both a little podless.

But together,
neither of us
is quite

   so

     alone.

AT THE DOCK

"I'm going to go down to the water,"
I tell Daddy.
He doesn't stop me,
though I know he knows
I *should* be checking Google Classroom
to see what assignments
my teachers have put up there.

I see her before my shoes even cross
onto the rough dock wood:
the tall gray fin,
shining in the morning sun.

Rose, *my* Rose, waiting just for me.

I stretch out on my belly on the dock
so that I can reach my arms
out over the water
and feel the smooth, smooth glide
of her rubber skin
as she lifts her head to nudge my fingers.

She hums at me, singing soft and low.

"Hey, girl," I say, whispering
even though it's just us out here.
"I missed you. No swimming today, though.
You and me, we've both got
lungs that kind of suck, right?"

I rub my hand up and down, up and down
the round hump of her melon
and Rose clicks gently, almost
like a purring cat.

Her broad grin is as huge and smiling as ever,
but even still, I can tell
there's something off about Rose today.
She's not playful and chuckling,
not trying to tease me into a game,
not splashing water at my face.
She's quieter, her movements small,
like she's as tired as I am.
I think of Dr. Zhao last week
of *lethargy*
and I wonder what she'd say
about Rose today.

I still my hand,
close my eyes,
and *listen*.

After three breaths, maybe four,
I swear I can feel it:
that pop-buzz-rush of connection.
Rose and I, linked
skin to skin, heart to heart.
I feel her boundless love, her joy,
the dolphin laughter that always seems
to lurk beneath her smile—
that's all there, but so is a heaviness
a leaden thread of sorrow
a weight that makes me catch my breath
and open up my eyes.

"I'm sorry," I say, though I don't know
if Rose can understand my words.
"You're not feeling so great, either.
But Dr. Zhao has a plan," I say.
"A plan to help you. Soon. I promise."
A plan to take you away,
I think, the unspoken words
twisting in my stomach.

Rose nudges me gently and blows
just a few drops of water up at me
like she's saying, *I know,*
like she's saying, *It makes me sad too.*
But before I take my hand away—
before our connection is severed—
there's one more thing Rose shows me:
a picture in my mind, clear
as my own memories, sharp
as the tang of salt water:
a pod of dolphins, just like her
l   e   a   p   i   n   g
into the sunshine, sea-foam streaming
from their silver tails.

      Her family.

        The ones
            she's lost.

LIKE A RED, RED ROSE

Daddy calls me inside then
and with one last pat, I say goodbye to Rose
and hurry to the house.
I'm almost to the back door when
the coughing fit starts:
like a feather tickling at my airways,
an itch starts deep down,
stealing my breath, making my lungs spasm
and cough and spasm
and cough and spasm until I start
to see black spots in my vision.
I hate when it gets like this—something lodged
so deep, so hard, I can't seem
to make it shift, but if I don't move it
I'll never stop the coughing.
I try to breathe slow and careful, try to stop
the spasms, try to catch my breath.
Finally, I cough again and boom:
deep inside my lungs,
in the dark mysterious passageways
where my breath lives,
I feel a catch, a wiggle, and out comes
a big old sticky blob
of disgusting gross horrendous yuck.

Daddy opens the back door
and hands me a tissue. "Sounds like things
       are starting to shift," he says cheerfully
as I spit (GROSS) into the tissue (GROSS)
       and throw it in the trash (GROSS).
"What color was it?" Daddy asks.
       GROSS, GROSS, GROSS.
Normal eleven-year-olds do not get quizzed
       about the color of their snot
by their parents, and I envy them. A lot.

       "Green," I say. "Dark."
"Hmm," says Daddy, who knows
       as well as I do that dark green
is the second-worst color you can cough up.

       I'm ready to be done
with the whole embarrassing conversation
       and go check Google Classroom
while I wait for Cricket to get home
       when I feel it *again*,
that tickle-itch, that need to cough and cough
       except this time, the coughs
are deep and wet, the kind my grandpa
       jokes sound like a barking seal.
Silent Daddy hands me another tissue,

but I can tell this time
a tissue won't be enough, so I run
into the bathroom,
turn on the light, and spit in the sink.

And what I see
is not dark green,
or even brown or black
but red, red, red
and it doesn't stop coming
no matter how much
I cough and spit
and cough and spit
and fill the bathroom sink
with bright red blood.

THINGS PARENTS DON'T SAY

Daddy is standing
in the bathroom doorway
when the coughing finally stops.
Together, we stare

at the little pool of red
swirling across white porcelain,
our silence heavy as a river.
Daddy doesn't say

Oh God, Penny, are you okay?
He doesn't say
What happened?
He just brings me a cup

filled to the brim with ice water
and as I drink, he eyes the sink,
silently estimating how many
tablespoons of blood are there.

Then he pulls me
into a big bear hug
and holds on to me like maybe
if he lets go, the world will end.

WHAT DADDY DOES

He washes out the sink,
refills my ice water
  (ice water helps
  to stop a lung bleed—
  which is a thing
  you know
  when you have CF),
gets me tucked into the recliner
with my purple rose blanket,
and then he calls Dr. Theo.

IT'S TIME

When Daddy's off the phone
I hear keys jangle in his hands.
"Dr. Theo says
it's time,"
Daddy says.
"Guess we get to take a trip
to Durham today."
I hear in his words all those things
parents don't say, either:
that *a trip to Durham* in this case
means *a trip to the doctor*
and maybe, maybe,
a stay in the hospital.

Some CFers are in the hospital a lot.
They get to know the nurses,
play pranks like
filling a sample cup with juice
instead of pee, then drinking it
when someone comes to pick it up.

(At least,
that's what it said on the
you don't have to be

so scared of the hospital
flyer Daddy gave me
last time I got admitted.)

But other CFers are like me—
we do okay at home
with breathing treatments
and antibiotics when we need them.
It's been two years
since I had to stay at the hospital.
Back in fourth grade
I got COVID-19
and it was the sickest I'd ever been.
I had to spend fourteen days
at Duke Hospital—
not once or twice, but *three times* that year.

But then things got better.
I started a new medication for CF
and haven't had to do IVs
for two whole years.

When Daddy says, *It's time*
I hear those words he isn't saying
and I know he means, *Go pack a bag.*

HEMOPTYSIS

The big medicalese word
for when you cough and it's bright red
blood rushing from a burst capillary in your lungs,
like the scariest horror movie
thing that could possibly happen
when you are only eleven years old
trying to figure out where you fit into the world
and most of the time would like to just forget
that you have something inside you
that rhymes with sixty-five roses
and, every now and then, blooms petal-red
in your bathroom sink.

Daddy says hemoptysis isn't always that bad,
that some CFers have it all the time.
Some get it every time they get their period.
Or if they lie down flat.
It's exactly like a bloody nose—it flows fast
and then stops slow.
By the time Daddy's off the phone
the stuff I'm coughing up is darker, old blood
mixed with mucus, a sign
my lungs are cleaning themselves out.
The worst is over.

Daddy says hemoptysis isn't always that bad—
but when it hasn't happened for two years
and you've already been on antibiotics
for four whole days,
hemoptysis means *it's time.*

DURHAM

Daddy calls Mama
fills her in
while he helps me pack a bag.
>   (*Not too much*,
>   he says.
>   *We can bring more later*
>   *if you have to stay.*)
He tells Mama
not to come home,
that he'll let her know
what happens.
Daddy lets me text Liana
everything that happened,
and before we leave
she texts back
during a passing period—
a flood of hearts
and kissy faces
and XOXOs
followed by
>   I love you, Penny
the first time in forever
she's called me my real name.

And that's the thing
that makes me almost cry.

It takes two hours to drive
to Durham.
Daddy plays podcasts
and tells jokes, and tries not
to ask too many times
if the blood is still coming up.

(It is.)

A HUMAN AT THE DOCTOR

CF visits always start with PFTs:
pulmonary function tests. You blow
    hard and fast into a machine
and it tells you how your lungs hold air.
    Everyone who works at the clinic
wears yellow sterile gowns and gloves and masks,
    keeping my CF germs
away from any other CFers who might be near.
    But if you've just had hemoptysis
they skip the PFTs, just in case
    they make you bleed again.
So Daddy and I get led right back
    to an exam room.

    We don't see Dr. Theo today.
She's too busy for last-minute visits,
    taking care of all her patients
in the outpatient clinic and the hospital, too.
    Instead, we see Nurse Jen.
She's wearing a white coat over her blue scrubs
    printed with unicorns and rainbows.
Nurse Jen has deep brown skin
    and the kind of voice

that makes you feel like maybe even bad things
        will be okay.
"Hi, Pen," she says with a smile.
        "Gotta say, I hoped
we wouldn't see you again this spring."
        (Mama and I
already drove here six weeks ago
        for my regular checkup.)
Nurse Jen listens to my lungs, has me tell her
        all the details of this morning.
"I'm so sorry, hon," she says, and her words
        make tears prick my eyes
as the fear-anger-worry-sorrow-grief
        I've had no time to really feel
threatens to well up deep inside.

        Nurse Jen takes a breath.
"Dr. Theo would really like you to do IVs.
        Fourteen days,
just like normal. I'm sorry, Penny.
        But it's time."

        Daddy clears his throat.
"Elizabeth and I were talking,"
        he says,
"and we thought maybe Penny could do IVs
        at home.

It's such a long drive out here for us,
     and with the timing—
Liz's spring break just ended—plus
     Penny would be more comfortable.
You know I'm an RT at CarolinaEast.
     We'd make sure
she gets extra treatments in, four times a day.
     She'd exercise
just like she would if she were inpatient.
     I can run her IVs.
And Penny's very mature. We trust her."

     Nurse Jen purses her lips,
takes a long moment to think about it.
     "You know we prefer
young CFers to do their IVs inpatient,"
     she says, then raises a hand
before Daddy can interrupt.
     "But I agree, Penny
is a unique case. Not every kid is lucky enough
     to have an RT for a dad.
I'll talk to Dr. Theo, but I think maybe
     we can get a PICC placed
this afternoon, then keep her for a night or two
     to get the dosage right,
and then you can finish up at home."

A little spark of hope
blooms in my chest. *Home!*
IVs are bad enough,
but if I didn't have to spend two weeks
in the hospital this time . . .
I think of Rose, of the team Dr. Zhao is sending.
Maybe I could get to say goodbye.

ONE OF THE LUCKY ONES, REPRISE

We leave the outpatient clinic
and go to the main hospital next door,
where they put a white bracelet
with my patient ID number on my wrist.
We wait for hours in the big atrium
for Nurse Jen to call Daddy
and say my room is ready.

I try to read a book while Daddy
pulls out his computer to get stuff done,
but it's hard to focus on the words
when my whole body feels
achy and sluggish and gross,
the way it always does after hemoptysis.

> All my life
> people have told me,
> *You're so lucky.*

I try to list the ways I'm lucky in my mind:
I've had two good, strong years.
I only coughed up
a few tablespoons of blood.
I won't have to stay two weeks this time.

But none of those things
make me feel any better
as I shift in my hard waiting-room chair
and watch the hours tick by.

All my life
people have told me,
You're so lucky—
But I don't feel
so lucky
now.

TOO YOUNG

When my room is finally ready
Daddy carries my bag onto the elevator
to the pediatric ward eight flights away.
There's a flurry of activity—
nurses pop in to take my temperature,
my blood pressure,
write a schedule on a whiteboard.
We wait *still more* hours
for the IV team to place a PICC line—
an extra-long, extra-strong IV
that starts inside my elbow and goes to my heart.
They give me meds to calm me down,
a little plastic cup of pink liquid
that burns my throat
but helps my heartbeat slow,
and squirt numbing cream on the soft skin
inside my elbow.

Here is a thing I know about Penny Rooney:
she really, really,
REALLY
hates
needles.

"I don't remember meeting you before,"
the IV nurse says
as she bustles around getting everything ready
and I try to look anywhere
but at the ginormous needle
she's going to stick me with.
"You seem pretty young for a PICC line!"

"She has cystic fibrosis,"
Daddy says.
The nurse's eyes go wide
behind her plastic face shield.
"Oh, wow!" she says. "You look so good
for a CF patient!"
I want to raise my eyebrows,
point out the obvious,
that *I'm sitting in a hospital right now,*
want to make her understand
the terror that still lingers inside me
after this morning.
The way every time I cough
my mouth fills with a nasty copper taste,
and I spit brown gunk into a tissue—
old blood, still seeping through my airways.
But I say nothing.

I'm used to this reaction,
used to being reminded
that I am one of the lucky ones.

I don't say anything back
because if I opened my mouth right now
what came out
would be one long, wordless scream.

MAYBE, BABY

I close my eyes as the nurse preps her tray full of stuff.
I breathe deep, try to imagine
I'm on the dock with Rose,
try to do anything to take my mind
off the EXTREMELY HUGE NEEDLE
that is about to be stabbed into my arm.
People always say I shouldn't mind needles like I do,
because you've had lots more experience than most kids,
but no matter how many times I've been stuck
for blood draws or shots or IVs,
it always makes my heart race and my head feel light.
I try to tune out the nurse's chatter,
let the meds she gave me fill my bloodstream,
let myself melt into the plastic hospital bed.

Daddy squeezes my hand tight
as the nurse washes off the numbing cream
and swabs up and down my arm
with spicy-scented chlorhexidine,
still talking the whole time
about this girl she knew once who died of CF.
Why do people do that?
Why does everyone seem to think
that what a person like me *most* wants to hear

the first time I meet anyone new
is all the people like me they knew who died?
I'm so annoyed by the chatter
I almost don't notice the first pinch
when the needle goes into my arm—
until the skin inside my elbow starts to *sting*,
even with all that numbing cream,
and I have to bite my lip to keep the tears in.

Maybe I'm a baby.
Maybe I should be braver, stronger.
Count my blessings.
It could be worse.
You could be sicker.
You could be dead.

Maybe all those things are true,
but none of them stop
the sting of that gigantic needle
or the bite as the nurse threads a plastic tube
up through my vein.
None of them change
the fact that I am the only almost-twelve-year-old
at my school
who's sitting here in a hospital bed
instead of in my Spanish class.

AT THE HOSPITAL

The evening is a blur—
exhaustion and coughing
nurses popping in
and medications
dripped through the PICC line
in my arm.
Cricket texts
as soon as she gets home
from school.

> My mom told me
> everything!
> I'm SO SORRY!
> Wish I could be there!

I wish she could, too.
Maybe this hospital room
wouldn't feel so cold
and lonely
if Cricket were beside me.

Instead, she's at home
packing up her life
while I'm hours away,
the time we have left

slip-

      slip-

           slipping

through our fingers.

         I wish that too,
         I send back.

Then again, maybe
it would be worse—
seeing her eyes go wide
at all the equipment
and white-clad doctors,
knowing that
as much as Cricket loves me
she'll never *really* understand
exactly what this feels like.

Mama and Liana call at dinnertime.
Daddy sets his tablet up
so we can see them both.
They ask a lot of questions
that Daddy mostly answers,
because I'm just

              too

                 tired.

"We should be out of here tomorrow,"
Daddy says two times
like he's reassuring himself
as well as them.
"I called out of work
for the next few days."
"Get some sleep," Mama tells me,
even though she knows
just as well as I do
that the hospital is the *worst* place
to try to sleep.
"See you soon, Little Moon,"
Liana says, and that does
make me crack a smile
because I don't know how in the heck
she can still think up new nicknames
after all this time.

BEEP, BEEP

It never gets really,
      truly
            dark
in a hospital room.
There are always
      lights
            noises
laughter from the nurses
down the hall,
      beep-
            beep-
beeping from the IV machine.
Daddy snoring
      on
            his cot.

Red lights, blue lights,
green lights
    blink
        blink
all around me, so that
every time
    I try
        to sleep
it feels like sleeping
in the middle of a
    freaking
        carnival
    ride.

TOO MUCH

I wake up at four a.m.
when a nurse turns on the light
right over my bed.
"Sorry!" she chirps.
"Time to check your levels!"

She winds a rubber strap
around my arm
pulls it tight
then holds up a needle.
The needle has an evil glint.

I do not like anything much
at four in the morning—
not nebulizers, not car alarms.
But a needle at four a.m.
is just too much.

The tears slip out before I know it,
splashing on the bright white
hospital blanket,
leaving twin spots of damp
seeping outward.

"It'll just be a little pinch,"
the nurse says.
"A big girl like you
can be brave, I know it!"
That just makes it worse.

The tears fall harder, faster.

"Ohhh," the nurse says,
her smile faltering
when she sees my face.

Across the room, Daddy stirs,
sits up slowly.

"We just need a tobra trough
so your doctor can make sure
the antibiotic dose is right,"
the nurse says. "Maybe
you could help, Dad?"

In one quick motion, Daddy is up
off the plastic recliner,
putting down the bed rail,
sitting on the edge of my bed.
His warm familiarity makes me cry harder.

"Let her take her time,"
Daddy tells the nurse.
"It's four in the morning.
She's had a long twenty-four hours.
It won't hurt to take some time."

He rubs my back
and lets the tears come
while the nurse hovers uncertainly
on the other side of my bed,
annoyance on her face.

SIXTY-FIVE ROSES

All my life,
everything
has been different
because of CF.

The pills I take
every time I eat,
trying to ignore
the cafeteria stares.

The way I can't
sleep over at Cricket's
without bringing
my neb and vest along.

The way Mama
hands me
protein shakes
with my breakfast.

The way our whole
year is shaped
around trips to the doctor
every three months.

Even my baby pictures—
the way they're so full
of tubes and wires,
you can hardly see my face.

All my life,
everything in it
has been different
because of CF.

But never has that
made me feel
as angry-sad-upset
as it does tonight.

WHAT I WANT TO DO

Usually I'm pretty good
at keeping a smile on

counting my blessings
being *mature*

just like Daddy
told Nurse Jen.

But at four a.m.,
crying so hard I shake,

I want to stand up
on this hospital bed

rip out my PICC line
and scream and scream

and scream some more
at every single person

who's ever told me
my CF is not so bad:

*THIS IS NOT WHAT
LUCKY LOOKS LIKE!*

WHAT I DO INSTEAD

Finally, finally, after maybe years,
the tears slow down.
I am all cried out,
a dry hole hot and crackling
inside my heart.
Slowly, slowly, I feel
my breathing ease, my shoulders
still after all that shaking.
Next to me, Daddy doesn't move,
even though he can't be comfortable.

I lean into him,
letting his big arms come around me,
his soft belly pillow my body.
I take a deep breath
and hold out my arm
for the nurse
to retighten her tourniquet.

The needle, when it comes,
is a quick fire,
stinging, stinging,
but then
it's done.

The nurse packs up her stuff,
turns off the light,
closes the door with a loud click.
And Daddy stays right there,
rubbing my back,
until I drift off to sleep.

CLOUDY WITH A CHANCE OF RAIN

The next day
the doctor on call
doesn't want to let us go.
"You'll have to do
two more sets of antibiotic levels
through home health care,"
he says, but Daddy says
that's fine,
Nurse Jen gave the okay,
we really, *really* want to go home.

I lie on the plastic bed
listening to them argue,
not sure if I would rather fall asleep
or cry.
If I were a weather forecast
I'd be *cloudy with a chance of rain.*
Finally the doctor
throws up his hands
and agrees to sign the discharge papers.

I'm in a fog all day
while they draw blood again to see

how much antibiotic is in my bloodstream.
(MORE NEEDLES. UGH.)
The medicine pumping
up to my heart
makes me feel sicker than I did before.
I flip through Netflix on the TV,
try to eat the cardboard hospital hamburger
on my lunch tray, even though
it tastes like greasy dirt.

I listen when the home health nurse
comes in, late in the afternoon,
to teach us how to use
the syringes, swabs, and pumps
we'll need to run my IVs at home.
Daddy rubs my back again,
gives my shoulder a little squeeze,
but even his warm, big hands
can't shake off
the cumulonimbus inside my head.

GOING HOME

I finally get discharged
at seven thirty that night.
Daddy grins as he packs up my stuff,
hefts the box from the home health nurse
onto a black wheelchair
like a cart.
"Everything in the hospital
takes a hundred times as long
as they say it will,"
he says.
"Ready to go home, Lucky Penny?"
Even if it still feels
as if all my luck's run out,
the word *HOME*
shines through
the clouds inside me
like a ray of sunlight blazing
through the gloom.

I sleep all the way home—
hardly waken when Daddy gently
shakes me, guides me
from the car,

up the steps,
in the door to our house.
I sleepwalk through Mama's hug
and a squeeze from Liana—
her eyes shiny with unshed tears.
I fall into bed with my clothes still on
and don't even notice
when Daddy comes in a few hours later
to run my midnight infusion.

HOME

WEDNESDAY

The next morning
I sleep through my six a.m. IV
and don't open my eyes until after ten,
sunshine striped hot and bright
across my bed.
I feel like I could sleep
a hundred years
while a hedge of roses grows around me.

Daddy's at the table when I drag myself
downstairs, his reading glasses
on his nose, papers spread around him.
"My supervisor's letting me clock in
a few hours from home
to catch up on paperwork," he says
cheerfully, like this
is the world's best news,
like taking off work to care
for his sick daughter is the coolest.

I rub my left arm where it's still sore
from yesterday's PICC placement.
At least at home, I don't have to stay

hooked up to an IV pole all the time—
my antibiotics come packed
in clear plastic balls, bigger than my fist,
and when it's time for an infusion
Daddy hooks one to a tube
and connects that to my PICC.
Once it's done, I'm free again,
just me and the little catheter
taped to my arm
that slips inside my vein.

"Oh," Daddy says, "Dr. Zhao emailed
this morning. She says they tracked Rose
down yesterday and successfully
gave her antibiotics.
Rose is still in Turtle Creek,
so today, Dr. Zhao will bring a boat our way
and coax her toward the Sound.
They'll be here after lunch."

Sadness and excitement
twist together in my heart.
Rose and me, both on medicine
to treat that *Pseudomonas aeruginosa*.
Rose and me, both back home
where we belong—

but don't we also belong together?
I close my eyes, reach inside,
for the thread of me that's tied to Rose.
She isn't nearby, but I can feel her anyway,
like firelight on my skin.
Don't go, I think. *Don't go.*

HOME IVS

Daddy spends the morning
going over our new routine:

Two IV antibiotics—
one every twelve hours
one every six,
which equals a *lot*
of infusions.
Six a.m., twelve p.m.,
six p.m., twelve a.m.:
Daddy marks the hours
on a whiteboard
just like the one they had
in the hospital.

Four breathing treatments—
double my normal
to help clean all that
icky junk
out of my lungs.

Daily exercise
because, as Dr. Theo says,
Exercise is airway clearance, too.

While Dr. Theo said
I *could* go back to school
if I felt up to it,
I can't imagine
trying to fit all these treatments
and infusions
and exhaustion
in with quizzes and
six hours in a hard school chair.
Keeping up with the assignments
my teachers post online
will be hard enough.

By the time I am done
with my first treatment
and breakfast
and half an hour
on the treadmill,
I am already ready
for a good, long NAP.

GOODBYE, GOODBYE

Dr. Zhao calls later, as Daddy and I
are finishing our lunch.
She says, "We're about five minutes away."

She says, "Our tracker shows
Rose is lingering near your place."
She says, "Now would be a good time to say goodbye."

I don't know if there's ever really
a good time to say goodbye.
Expected or not, goodbyes hurt.

It hurt Monday, to say goodbye when Liana
went back to school and I didn't.
To be stuck here, blank-slate Penny, all alone.

It hurt to say goodbye to my house, my bed,
when we went to the hospital
and didn't know how long I'd have to stay.

It hurts, too, when we put away our lunch things
and walk down to the water,
and Daddy puts his arm around me as we go.

It hurts when we get to the dock and see Rose,
ready and waiting for us, like she knew
we were coming, which of course she did.

It hurts when I crouch on the dock—
no lying down this time, in case
it triggers the blood again,

reach my good arm (the one without the PICC)
over the water, feel her smooth shining skin
under my fingers for the last time.

It hurts when she does her cat-purr clicking,
when she splashes me gently,
when she beams that love right to my heart.

I don't say anything out loud. Just close my eyes
and let my hand rest on Rose's melon,
remembering every perfect moment.

I see again that picture:
a pod of dolphins, playing in the waves,
and I know that Rose is hurting, Rose is lonely, too.

But she bats my hand, soft and playful,
and without words I know she's saying,
But I'm still going to miss you.

And that makes it hurt a little less.

DOLPHIN HERDING

Dr. Zhao and her interns come up
on a small boat.
"We're hoping to entice Rose downstream
with a combination of treats and novelty,"
she says. She points to a cooler
I assume is full of stinky dead fish.
"We'll try to coax her toward us,
then play with her a bit.
Hopefully when we turn our engine on,
she'll try to race us back.
Boat wakes are catnip for dolphins.
They love to surf them."

"That seems easy," says Daddy.
"This whole time all the dolphin needed
was a boat wake to surf?"

Dr. Zhao laughs, her eyes crinkled in a smile.
"I guess we'll see," she says, "in an hour or two."
She tells us we can stay and watch awhile,
but asks that we move back from the dock
so Rose won't be distracted.
"She's built such a beautiful relationship

with you—with Penny especially—
and that might render us less interesting."
Daddy sets two camp chairs on the lawn
and I sit, feeling the invisible string
between my heart and Rose

s   t   r   e   t   c   h

longer   and   longer.

Goodbye, goodbye, goodbye, I think.
Goodbye, miracle friend.
Goodbye, my Rose,
whose lungs suck just like mine.

The scientists toss Rose some fish,
get her circling their boat. One of them
splashes water at her,
and Rose splashes back.
Before long, she's playing with them,
squeaking and clicking,
rising up so Dr. Zhao can pet her, just like I do.
The doctor rubs her round head,
coos softly at her, then hand-feeds her
a fish from a different container.
Another antibiotic, I bet.

At least I don't have to take my meds
stuffed into disgusting stinky fish!
Rose doesn't mind.
She swallows that medicated fish
like it's ice cream in the summer.

After a while, Esteban the intern
slowly starts the motor on the boat.
Rose leaps away.
"She definitely doesn't like motors,"
Esteban says, laughing.
But Rose warily swims closer,
liquid eyes curious
above the waterline.
Esteban motors forward slowly.
The river splits behind the boat,
little waves running away from each other
toward opposite banks.
Rose follows, slow and skittish.
"I guess that's it, then," Daddy says.
We watch as Esteban slowly ups his speed
until the boat is clipping downstream.
Rose hangs back, but still
follows   at a distance,
splashing in the boat's wake, letting herself
be herded, exactly as Dr. Zhao hoped.

Goodbye, I think again as the boat
gets smaller and smaller, Rose behind.

There's an ache when I take a breath,
    and this time
        I don't think
            it's from CF.

CHIRP

Cricket comes over later, after school.
The IVs make me foggy and tired
so we lie on the couch,
legs piled together like spaghetti,
and watch *Moana* and then *Luca*,
which is about sea monsters.
My favorite part is the big fisherman
who was born with one arm.
He's different—
      like Rose,
      like me,
but nobody ever thinks it's weird
or makes fun of him
or asks him where his arm went.

Kind of like how Cricket
isn't bothered when Daddy comes over
and hooks up my next infusion,
flushing my PICC line with saline
and then screwing on the long tube
connected to the clear plastic ball
that pushes medicine
s   l   o   w   l   y

into my arm.
She just hands him the alcohol wipes
when he asks for them
and then pretends to balance the IV ball
on her head until I laugh so hard
I start to cough.

That is why Cricket is my best friend:
because no matter what's happening at my house
she acts like it's no big deal,
like I am exactly as
       cool
       fun
       interesting
as she's always thought I was.

FORTUNATELY, UNFORTUNATELY

There are two things waiting
when I wake up on Thursday morning.
The first is a home health nurse
with two giant cardboard boxes
of infusion supplies
and an order from the doctor
to draw my blood *again*.

The second is a message on Daddy's phone.
It's Dr. Zhao.
"Unfortunately, we weren't able
to get Rose far enough today,"
Dr. Zhao's recorded voice says
when Daddy plays the message.
"She followed us almost to the mouth
of Turtle Creek, then lost interest
and returned upstream.
She's consistently spooked by motors—
must've had a bad encounter.
I'm concerned
about her growing lethargy,
how long she's been in low salinity.
Today we'll put our heads together
to see if we can figure out a new plan."

Technically
it is *fortunate*
that my living room
is full of IV supplies
that will
make me better
and *unfortunate*
that Rose is lurking
in our river still,
but I have to admit
it does not feel
that way,
which is the funny thing
about *fortune*.

A GARDEN OF ROSES

I do not cry this time
when the home health nurse
draws my blood

with her wicked, shining needle.
Even when she digs
and digs to find a vein

and then has to pull it out
and stick me a second time,
I blink back the tears

before they can roll down.
Daddy watches me
and when the nurse leaves

he gives me a hug.
"I know it's hard," he says,
and his gentle words

undo the knot tied in my chest
so I can't stop the tears anymore.
Daddy holds me while I cry.

When I've used up all my tears,
Daddy says, "Lucky Penny,
I have an idea. Grab your phone."

I hand it to him. He turns it on,
then downloads a pic-sharing app
that *he* always said

I'm not allowed to have.
"Your mom and I talked it over,"
he says at my skeptical look.

"We know this week
has been tough.
We think that this might help."

He clicks the magnifying glass
at the bottom of the screen,
types in *#cysticfibrosis*.

I gasp at the images
that fill the phone
square after square.

There are grown-ups,
little kids,
almost-teens my age.

Blond, brunette.
Smiling, frowning.
Casual, posing.

> *But*
> *they*
> *are*
> *all*
> *like*
> *me.*

Some lie in hospital beds.
Others have oxygen looped beneath noses.
Some hold up arms with PICC lines.

In one square, I see a girl
maybe my age,
thumbs-up to the camera,

a bright pink vest wrapped around her,
a nebulizer in her mouth,
mist curling up.

"Your mama and I were thinking,"
Daddy says as I scroll through.
"Some CF friends would be good.

We agreed you can create
an account here, as long
as we have access to it.

Maybe you can't surround
yourself with CF friends
you can touch—

but right here on this phone
there's a community
waiting for you, Pen."

And even though I don't yet know
any of the names
of the people in those squares,

seeing them is enough
to make my coughing hurt
a little less, the soul-deep weariness

from the IVs coursing
through my bloodstream
just a little lighter.

THE SECOND *F* IS IMPORTANT

Cricket comes again that afternoon
with a story
about how she sat in my seat in homeroom,
right in front of Lyla Rain,
and how Lyla Rain tapped her
on the shoulder
and said Cricket's braid was beautiful.

"It *is* beautiful,"
I say, because Cricket's mom
has watched a hundred YouTube tutorials,
and Cricket's silky hair is twisted
in a spiral crown around her head.
But I know by Cricket's secret, shy smile
that Lyla Rain's *beautiful*
means something different than mine.

I show her the social media account
Daddy helped me set up this morning:
@65rosesforpenny.
I already uploaded a photo of me
holding one of my IV balls.
I show her the CFers I've already followed,

my news feed full of
smiles and sadness,
hospital hallways and vest selfies.

"I'll ask my mom if I can get it, too,"
says Cricket.
"It'll help us keep in touch, when . . .
well, you know."
The knowing
is a heavy lump inside me.

"I don't want you to go," I say,
even though I know it's the kind of thing
Mama always says is
true, but not so helpful.
"I don't want to go," Cricket says,
and we lean our heads together, her light brown
hair mingling with my dark.

"You know no matter how far away I am,"
Cricket says,
"you're always going to be
my very best friend, right?
*BFF*s. Best friends forever.
That second *F* is important. Don't forget."

"I won't," I say. Because Cricket's right—
no matter how far away Virginia is,
we will always be BFFs,
Cricket'n'Penny,
two halves of the same whole.

AN IDEA

"Hey,"
Cricket says.
"Could we go
outside,
see if
your dolphin's
there?"

"Sure,"
I say,
and then
even through
the foggy IV brain,
the best idea
in history
blooms
in my mind.

I grab
Cricket's
hand
and pull her
downstairs.

Daddy's
in the kitchen,
humming
while he gets
started
on dinner.
Mama's
on the phone
with some parent
who can't
wait
until morning.

"Hey!"
I say.
"Can Cricket
and I
take a kayak out?"
Daddy squints
at us
a long minute.
"We'll wear
life jackets,
and take
a phone,
and won't

go far,"
I promise.

"Fine," Daddy says.
"But get Liana
to help
pull it out.
You're not
supposed
to be lifting.
And wrap your arm!"

Cricket
and I
look at each other
and
can hardly keep
from squealing.

THE KAYAK

Liana grumbles, but goes out to help
Cricket with the kayak anyway,
since my PICC line means
no heavy lifting.
While they get the boat down
to the water, I pull out the Press'n Seal,
rip off a big strip, and wrap it carefully
around my PICC arm.
It sticks to my skin better
than regular old plastic wrap,
which makes it easier. It's what we do
anytime I need a shower, too.
I seal it up with medical tape, so the whole thing
is wrapped up tight and waterproof,
then run out to the dock,
not even caring that it makes me cough.

Cricket and Liana have the tandem kayak
all ready. It's the one
Daddy and Liana paddle
when they go on their yearly camping trips,
exploring up and down the Neuse.
Once, when I was little,

I asked if I could go with them
when they went for two whole nights,
camping beside the river way upstream,
sleeping in a tent that packs down so small
you can hold it in one hand.
Mama hugged me and said those trips
were Daddy and Liana's thing,
that we couldn't fit all my therapy stuff
on the tiny kayak, and the campsites
wouldn't have electricity.
But she promised that she and I
could pop popcorn and watch a movie *both* nights.
That was fun, for sure—
but it didn't stop the sting of jealousy
when Daddy and Liana came back
sunburned and grinning, full
of stories I could never be a part of.

Cricket's already in the boat,
life jacket clipped,
a paddle in her hand.
Liana holds up a second jacket.
"Go row that boat, Goose,"
she says as I slip my arms inside,
and it makes me remember
that Daddy isn't the only one who's sat

with Liana in that tandem kayak.
When we were younger,
we used to paddle it together while we sang
"Row, Row, Row Your Boat"
in an endless round.

ON THE WATER

In another breath
I'm in the kayak
and Liana's waving from the dock.
Cricket and I dip our paddles in,
then giggle when they accidentally clack together.
Once we've found our rhythm, we glide
into the center of the creek,
paddles slicing through the navy water.
It feels different out here,
even though we're barely around
the first bend in the creek.
Being on the water like this is
wild, quiet,
like me and Cricket are a part
of this whole beautiful wide watery world.

"Where do you think she might be?"
Cricket asks.
I take a deep breath. Will Cricket, with her brilliant brain
that handles numbers like they're nothing,
think I'm weird? Making things up?
"I think I can get her to come to us,"
I say all in a rush.

Cricket's forehead wrinkles, but I close my eyes,
breathe soft and slow,
reach for the thread between me and Rose.

Rose, I think. *My friend.*
Come play with us?

For a while, nothing really happens.
Tiny ripples lap the kayak sides.
A turtle raises its knobby head to the surface near the bank.
A pair of kingfishers fight
in the trees above us, each trying to rattle-squawk
louder than the other.
The furrow in Cricket's forehead deepens.

AND THEN—

Just as I've given up—
she comes. *Rose. My friend.*
Rolling through the water like a dream,
she knocks into our kayak so we gently rock.

Cricket screams.
I laugh
and reach out my hand to rub Rose's head.
"It's okay," I say to Cricket. "She won't hurt us."
Cautiously, Cricket reaches out, too.
Rose lets her run a wondering finger
across her melon.
"Cricket, meet Rose," I say.
"Rose, this is Cricket, my best friend on land."
Rose clicks at us
and splashes just a little bit,
though I notice
she doesn't get water anywhere near my wrapped-up arm.

Somehow, she knows.

"Try paddling again," I say to Cricket.
As soon as we start gliding, Rose is there

swimming alongside—
Now on the left,
now on the right,
weaving through our ripples. *Playing.*
We've only gone the length of a house or two
when Rose pulls ahead and

                              !

                         S

                    P

               A

          E

     L

from the water, shedding sparkling droplets,
then dives sleekly back into the creek.

MAGIC

"Wow," Cricket breathes.
"This is amazing."

"I know," I say
as our paddles dip in and out

and Rose swirls
through the water beside.

"It was almost
like magic," Cricket says,

"the way she came
just when we wanted her."

"I know," I say, and paddle,
the burn in my PICC arm

swallowed by
the whole-body glow

I feel with Rose so close.

A MIRACLE FOR THREE

We paddle a little while longer—
not too far, like we promised Daddy,
especially since the farther we go
the more my arm hurts.
Rose stays with us the whole time—
bobbing and playing, every now and then
bumping into us to get us gently rocking,
but never so hard that we might fall in.
Cricket pulls out her phone
and records a video:
our kayak slicing through the water,
Rose keeping time beside us.
"This is the most amazing thing I think
I've ever experienced,"
says Cricket when she puts the phone away,
and I think, *Me too.*

A NEW IDEA

Finally Rose swims away downstream
and Cricket and I head home.
When Daddy comes to drag the kayak to the shed,

we show him the video.
"Whoa," Daddy says, watching it twice through.
"She really tracked you, didn't she."

Cricket and I exchange a glance.
Neither of us know how to put into words
the way Rose came because *I* called.

"Can you send this to Dr. Zhao?"
I ask Daddy.
"I think . . . I think I've got a new idea."

THE JOURNEY

WORTH TRYING

That night, after I've finished evening treatments
and gotten ready for bed,
Mama and Daddy *both* come
to set up my bedtime IV infusion.
Mama settles into my desk chair while Daddy
perches on the edge of my bed,
swabbing the end of my PICC line with alcohol
before he squeezes in a syringe of saline
to clean out the line.
I can feel the saline rushing through the PICC,
cold under my skin. I can smell it too,
a stinging plastic scent all around me
that means it's in my bloodstream.

"Listen, Penny," Daddy says.
"I talked to Dr. Zhao this evening, about Rose.
I sent her the video of you and Cricket.
She said she's noticed
how fond Rose seems to be of you. She says
dolphins aren't that different from dogs—
sometimes they create a special bond
with certain humans."

I think of the way Rose and I always seem
to know where the other is.
The way she almost seems to *talk* to me sometimes,
and understand what I'm saying, too.
Maybe that's what magic looks like to grown-ups—
something science can explain.

"I told Dr. Zhao your idea," Daddy continues.
"That you go with her
when she tries to take Rose home again."
Mama clears her throat.
"I was a little skeptical at first," she says,
"but your daddy talked me through it, and I can see
how it might work."

Daddy swabs the PICC again
and hooks the antibiotic ball up.
"Dr. Zhao thinks your idea is worth trying.
Soon—maybe this weekend—
she'll come back here, try to lead Rose home again.
But this time, she'll have *you* on the boat, too.
You'll get a chance to feed Rose some treats,
play with her a bit, and hope
that when the boat starts up, she'll follow you."

I think again of this afternoon with Cricket,
of Rose leaping from the water like joy itself.
"I think we should take a kayak," I say,
even though I know it sounds ridiculous,
even though I have no idea how many miles
I'd have to paddle, even though
the IV exhaustion hasn't left, and my PICC arm
still feels sore. "You saw that video, Daddy. You saw
how close she stayed, how much she loved it.
I think I need to be down in the water *with* her.
Not up on some noisy motorboat.
Even Dr. Zhao says Rose hates motors."

"No way," Mama says.
"Penny, honey, there's too much risk
of getting your arm wet—and you know
you aren't supposed to lift too much.
Dr. Theo would never sign off on miles of kayaking."
"But it's exercise!" I say. "You know
what Dr. Theo always says:
Exercise is airway clearance.
In fourth grade when I went to the hospital,
they sent me to the gym every single day.
And it wouldn't have to be me alone—
somebody could come with me, in the tandem,
so I didn't have to paddle too much."

I think of Liana and "Row, Row, Row Your Boat,"
even though I know the trip
would be too far without a real adult.

But Daddy could do it with me.

"I'll talk to Dr. Zhao," Daddy says,
cleaning up all the used syringes and half-dry swabs
and tossing them into my bedside trash.
"We'll see what she says."
Mama stands, comes to kiss my forehead.
"Go to sleep now," she says. "Maybe
you'll dream of Rose."

FRIDAY MORNING

By the time I wake up—
hours after Daddy came in
to do my six a.m. infusion—
Mama's at the kitchen table.
Friday's one of Daddy's work days, and since
he's already taken off two this week,
Mama got permission
to do her school secretary work from home.

"I talked to Dr. Zhao this morning,"
Mama says. "She agrees the kayak
might keep Rose more engaged—but, Penny,
I don't know. It's fifteen miles of paddling
to where Dr. Zhao wants to go.
I just think that's too much."

"Daddy's done longer than that," I say.
"Last summer he and Liana
went all the way up
past New Bern. Thirty miles or more!"
Mama's lips pinch.
"That's not quite the same," she says,
and I know in between the words
are all the things she *doesn't* say:

Liana is older, bigger, stronger.
Liana doesn't have CF.

"It didn't hurt my arm *too* much
when Cricket and I kayaked yesterday,"
I press. "If we go slow
and take lots of breaks, I *know* I can do it.
What does Daddy think?"

Mama smiles, a rueful grin
that says, *You know how Daddy is.*
"Your daddy spent the morning on his GPS app,
mapping it all out and planning snacks
to take along," she says, and there's something
in her voice that gives me a glimmer
of hope that even though she's saying,
I don't think so, she might be gearing up to say *okay*.
"I'll think about it, Pen. I sent a message
to Dr. Theo, asking what she thinks."

"She might say yes," I say.
"She always says it's important
for me to get to be a kid as much as possible."

The question is
if *being a kid* conflicts
with *staying healthy,*
which will Dr. Theo pick?

TALKING TO ROSE

After I've done my first treatment
eaten breakfast
and walked thirty minutes on Mama's treadmill
(because exercise makes strong lungs),
I go outside to look for Rose.
Liana stops me by the back door
and shyly asks, "Can I come this time?"
We sit together on the dock,
and while we wait for Rose to wander by,
Liana sings an old round
she learned at summer camp:
Rose,   Rose,
         Rose,   Red,
the music weaving through the treetops
and shimmering on the water.
After a few minutes we see Rose's fin
cutting strong and sharp through Turtle Creek.
"Hey, girl," I say, stretching my good arm out
to run my fingers across her skin.
Liana's hand joins mine,
my sister's face painted in wonder.
I use my other hand to snap a photo of us three—
Liana and me on the dock, Rose in the water—
to post online later.

"What do you think of all this planning, huh?"
I murmur to Rose.
"Are you ready to head home?"

"She'll miss you," Liana says,
scratching under Rose's chin.
"I don't have to be a dolphin whisperer to see it."

Rose seems perkier today:
a little more sparkle in her liquid eyes,
a little more playful when she bats my hand.
Maybe the antibiotic Dr. Zhao gave her is helping.
I can't tell if mine is yet.
It's hard to know, when the IVs themselves
make me feel like something yucky you might find
on the bottom of your shoe.
My cough is still deep and heavy,
but the crackle in my lungs is gone
and I haven't had more hemoptysis.

I close my eyes and picture our blue tandem kayak,
the way Rose swam with me and Cricket yesterday.
I picture me and Daddy—
him in back to do the steering—
paddling down Turtle Creek and out
to the huge expanse of the Neuse River.
What do you *think, girl?* I ask Rose silently.

Will it work? Will you come with us?

I've hardly finished my silent question
when Rose sends a picture back to me.
The same one as before: a pod of dolphins,
all together in what must be the Pamlico Sound,
sun shining on their silver skin
water sheeting from them as they leap and play.

I may not speak dolphin, but
I have a feeling Rose is trying to say
she's ready to head home.

NICE TO MEET YOU

That afternoon
when I sit
to do my third
breathing treatment
of the day
I have a notification
on my phone.
Someone
has followed me back—
@yoursaltysophia.
Her grid is full
of photos:
a girl with dark red hair
and laughing eyes.
Some are just selfies
like you'd see
on anyone's account,
but others
show her holding up
a glucose monitor
or doing PFTs
at her hospital.
13 years old
her bio says.

CF Fighter 🌷
CF-related diabetes 💉:
Double delta f508 🔗
South Carolina girl
And when I check
my IG in-box
there is a message
from @yoursaltysophia:
Hi! That pic of you
with the dolphin
is amazing!
Nice to meet you! 😃

SOPHIA

I spend my whole treatment time
messaging Sophia.
She tells me about her dog, Boberry,
and how he always keeps her company
when she does treatments
and warns her if her blood sugar's low.

She says she hasn't been on IVs
in a few years but still has PICC scars
like little moons
on the insides of her elbows.
I tell her about my hemoptysis Monday
and how exhausted IVs make me

and even tell her a little about Rose—
how Rose has *Pseudomonas aeruginosa*
in her lungs, just like we do.
Sophia says her favorite book
is called *Planet Earth Is Blue*
and I tell her about the poetry slam

Ms. Berman's planning
and how much I hate Google Classroom.
I almost don't notice

how long my treatment takes
because my heart is so filled up
with a warm, excited glow.

For so long, I've had no one
else like me to talk to.
But Sophia understands
midnight treatments
and the sting of IV lines

and what it feels like
to have sixty-five roses
in your DNA.

THE NEW PLAN

Cricket comes over
after school and stays for dinner.
I sit at the table
with a bag slung over my shoulder
to hold the IV ball
that's finishing my evening infusion
while Liana passes pizza slices around.
Daddy gets home from work,
and after a super-quick shower
he joins us at the table and announces:
"I've talked to Dr. Zhao,
and she thinks the kayak is a good idea."

Mama purses her lips tight
and I can tell she's worrying,
but she admits
that Dr. Theo replied to her message
only a few minutes ago.
"Dr. Theo says as long as Penny
isn't paddling so much it strains her arm,
and as long as she can fit in
all her treatments and rest up well after,
she thinks the trip sounds doable."

"What do *you* think, Liz?"
Daddy asks, meeting Mama's eyes.
Mama shrugs. "You're still my baby, Penny,"
she says softly. "I'll always worry
about you. But I know how much
this means to you, and I think
if Daddy's with you, it'll be okay."

"WOO-HOO!" Liana whoops,
shaking her hips in a funny chair dance,
and in that moment, every little bit
of envy or frustration I have ever had
about the things Liana can do that I can't
dissolves into warm, glowing love
for my big sister.

Daddy says
Dr. Zhao wants to try
the new plan on Monday
since I won't be at school
at least until the IVs end
nine days from now.
She'll come up with a small boat
at eight thirty in the morning,
so I have time for my first IVs
and a breathing treatment, too.

Daddy and I will paddle
in the blue tandem kayak
and Dr. Zhao will follow at a distance,
so her motor won't scare Rose.
We'll have walkie-talkies
if we need to get in touch.

After dinner, Daddy spreads
a map across the table.
"Here's Turtle Creek," he says, pointing
at a little blue ribbon winding off the Neuse.
He traces a line out of our creek,
down the big river,
eventually ending up on the other bank.
"This is the route we think we'll follow,"
he says. "Right to where the river opens up
into the Pamlico Sound.
We'll dock in this town here,
and then Mama and Liana
will bring the truck to get us home."

"How long will this whole thing take?"
Liana asks.
Daddy shrugs. "There's a lot of variables,
but I'm planning six hours
to go about fifteen miles.

One mile to the mouth of Turtle Creek,
then fourteen down to the Neuse mouth,
where it turns into the Sound."

Cricket bounces in her seat.
"This is SO EXCITING," she says.
"I can't believe you're really doing it!
I wish I could be there."
I wish Cricket could be, too,
but there's no room for three in a tandem
and besides, Dr. Zhao said it's best
not to overwhelm Rose with too many humans.
"I'll take lots of pictures and videos,"
I promise—

and I try not to think
of how when Cricket moves
(in only *five* weeks now!)
pictures and videos will be all we have.

THE WEEKEND

Is slow as molasses rolling from a jar.
Mama says
I need to rest and concentrate

      on treatments
      and exercise
      and getting well,

so Monday doesn't make me any sicker.
She sighs and says,
"I still can't believe we're doing this,"
but she's smiling, too,
and when she pulls me into a hug
and plants a gentle kiss on my hair,
she adds in a whisper,
"I'm really proud of you, Penny.
This is a brave and wonderful thing."

And as she lets me go, I think
I might be able to put a finger
on what I know about Penny Rooney.

CHURCH

Mama says I don't have to go to church
on Sunday. But to everyone's surprise,
including mine, I wake up
feeling not so bad—my cough is
gentler, doesn't shake my body,
and the fevery heat that's danced across
my skin all week has cooled.
For the first time since I got sick,
I can take a good, deep breath, feel the air
go all the way to the bottom of my lungs.
I decide I want to go
mostly because I'm tired of the house.
But when we get there and slide
into the padded pew, it feels nice,
sitting in the quiet chapel,
listening to the organ prelude music,
with Daddy's soft bulk on one side of me
and Liana's lemon-scented shampoo smell
on the other.
Liana wraps her arm around me
and we sing the hymns together—
my voice weak and cracking,
hers smooth and strong as water.

For so many weeks I've felt
adrift, caught up a lonely creek,
bound into a body full of pain and sickness—
a podless girl, full of questions nobody can answer.
But this morning, with my family all around me,
things are different. I think of storms
on the river, and how when they're over
the sunlight washes everything in gold,
each leaf and water droplet made anew.

BUDDING

Mama and Daddy
say for now, I can use social media
    while I do treatments—
which feels like *all* the time on this
    home IV schedule.
Sunday after church, I get a notification
    that I've got
two new followers: @cffoundationcarolinas,
    which is full of posts
about fundraisers and people with CF
    right here in NC,
and @cfmaddy, who is just my age
    and lives in California.
My heart feels like it's growing
    three whole sizes
with every new CF friend I find—
    like some part of me
I didn't know was missing, exploding
    into life
a little more each time.

MONDAY MORNING

I'm too excited to calm down when it's time
for bed on Sunday night
so Mama gives me Benadryl to help me sleep.
"Dr. Theo suggested it," she says,
"so you're not too tired tomorrow."
I swallow the pink pills down.
The pre-bed hug she gives is extra tight.
My sleep is fast and deep and dreamless,
and when I wake up Monday morning I feel
like the rays of sunshine flooding through my window
are seeping right inside me,
filling my lungs and fingers and toes
with brilliant golden light.

I'm still not ready to say goodbye to Rose—
the thought sits hard and heavy
behind my sternum.
But for now, the excitement of this magic
miracle adventure, these hours
I'll get to spend beside my friend—
that is enough.

Daddy helps me run my early-morning infusion
while I pour a bowl of cereal
and count out my morning enzymes.
The two and a half hours it takes
for the antibiotics to push their way out of the IV balls
have never, ever felt so long.

My whole body buzzes as I do my vest
and I can hardly concentrate on Instagram or books
or homework or *anything*—
because inside, I'm already out there
   on the water
   with Rose
feeling the magic between us swirl and sing.
Mama gives me ibuprofen when I've finished
to help keep my arm from getting too sore
and runs over our checklist once again:

> *Keep your arm wrapped tight.*
> *Stay out of the water.*
> *Let Daddy paddle when you're tired.*
> *If your PICC bleeds AT ALL, abort.*
> *Take your inhaler, just in case.*
> *Don't forget to drink plenty of Gatorade!*
> *We don't want your electrolytes to drop.*
> *Here—maybe you should take*
> *a few salt pills, too, just in case.*

Daddy comes up and puts a big, soft hand
on my shoulder. "She's gonna be just fine, Liz,"
he says, and the pride in his voice
when he says that
makes me glow from my head right down.

PREPARATIONS

By the time I've finished my breathing treatments,
Mama and Daddy have almost everything all ready:
sandwiches and snacks and lots of Gatorade,
sunscreen and hats and sunglasses for us both,
a whole roll each of Press'n Seal and medical tape.
Mama helps me wrap my arm with plastic double-thick,
until I feel like a robot who crinkles when she moves.

Liana gives me a big squeeze before her bus comes
and says, "You're a rock star, you know that, sis?"
I feel the warmth of her words down to my toes.
I wave out the window as she climbs onto her bus,
glad that Liana Rooney is a part of my pod.

Finally, FINALLY, we hear the pulsing hum
of a motorboat echoing from our backyard.

DR. ZHAO AND THE INTERNS

Are smiling
from the deck
of their little boat.
They look hopeful,
excited,
like they think
this might

                    just

                          work.

CALLING

Mama's going into school late today
and taking off work early
so she and Liana can come to pick us up.
She watches now
as Daddy and I snap our life jackets
pick up our paddles
and climb into the kayak.

Daddy gets in first, steadying it
so that it doesn't rock when I climb in.
My wrapped-up arm feels stiff and hot,
but I don't care at all.

Rose isn't here—
Dr. Zhao checks her tracker,
says Rose is lingering upstream.
"We could try to track her down," she says,
her excitement dimming.

"No," I say. "Let's wait a little."
Everyone falls silent,
the only sound the creek lapping at our boats,
the gobble-cry call of an egret downstream.

I close my eyes, just like I did
last week with Cricket,
and I call my friend.

Rose.
I picture her swimming
around the kayak.
Rose.
I think of the smooth silk
of her silver skin.
Rose.
I remember what it felt like
to swim beside her.
Rose.
And finally, I think of *her* picture:
a pod of dolphins in a sparkling sea.

And that is when she comes—
rolling through the water like she's been waiting,
waiting for my call.

LAUNCH

Rose comes to me first.
I reach a careful hand
over the water,
stroke her head.
For the last time?
Mama waves from the dock
as Daddy and I
dip our paddles in
and start to stroke.
When we've gone
two house lengths
I hear the soft purr
of Dr. Zhao's motorboat
start up behind us.
Rose keeps close,
just like she did last week
with Cricket and me,
diving and twirling
through the ripples we make.
"Wow," Daddy breathes.
"She's really beautiful, Penny."
"I know," I say,
and it feels like maybe

my heart will burst
right out of my chest
and beat into the sunny sky
like a butterfly.

TURTLE CREEK

The first mile is quiet.
Turtle Creek is calm and smooth,
    only our kayak
rippling the glassy surface.
    Only the faint hum
of Dr. Zhao's motor way behind us
    breaking the silence.
Every now and then a fish will jump,
    or a tiny turtle
poke up its head. The whole world
    feels hushed,
like it's holding its breath for us,
    like getting Rose home
is so important, all of Turtle Creek
    will help.

THE FIRST MILE

Daddy guessed it would take us
about twenty minutes to paddle to the creek mouth,
and sure enough, when the wide, wide river
comes into view, his watch says
it's just shy of nine.
The Neuse River is wide as a lake
sparkling in the sun. Right here,
the river is almost four miles across.
The other shore is just a watercolor smudge—
green-gray painted trees
wavering in shifting sunlight.

"How's it going?" Daddy asks,
looking at my plastic PICC arm.
I shrug. My muscles ache a little, but so far
not too bad. "I think I can keep going,"
I say. "It only hurts a tiny bit."
Daddy hands me my water bottle
and two salt pills, then a fruit bar.
With CF, every time you sweat
you lose a hundred times the salt
a normal person would.
"I just thought of something," I say

as I wash the pills down with water. "Rose—
she's sick because the water here is brackish, right?
She needs salt, just like me."

Daddy laughs. "You're right," he says. "Now,"
he adds, "don't push too hard.
We've got a lot of hours yet."
I stretch both arms out wide, yawn,
rub my bicep above the PICC line, nod.

Behind us, Dr. Zhao and the interns
cut the motor and idle slowly closer,
giving Rose her space as the dolphin
swirls around our kayak.
From her boat, Dr. Zhao gives me a thumbs-up.
I close my eyes and think again of Rose's pod,
all those dolphins together in the sunlight.
Do you miss them? I ask inside my mind.

Rose surfaces and makes a keening sound—
one I've never heard before.
I'm flooded with her memories:
silver skin on silver skin,
games played in pink dawn's light.

"Whoa," Daddy says. "What's that about?"
"She's sad," I say. "She's ready to go home."
Emotion swirls through me—
mine this time, not Rose's.
Excitement, relief, fear, sadness, joy,
one big hurricane of feelings, wide and deep
as the river itself.

LEAVING TURTLE CREEK

We steer around docked sailboats
as our creek opens into the Neuse.
And between one breath and the next we're there,
in the big river,
water all around us.
It's so broad, waves wash against the shore,
crest and curl like a tiny ocean.
The river's surface glitters darkly
and feels as broad and deep as dreams.
Rose follows us out of the creek mouth,
and maybe I'm imagining it—
but she seems to be moving faster, seems
a little lighter as she plays in our wake.
Just as we turn the kayak
so we're facing downstream,
toward the Pamlico Sound—
Rose dives down deep, then surges up—
and LEAPS right over the kayak's nose.
I laugh as droplets rain down on me and Daddy,
pinging on my wrapped-up arm.

The walkie-talkie clipped to my life jacket crackles
and I hear Dr. Zhao,
echoing my words to Daddy earlier.
"Rose is ready to go home."

TOGETHER

After leaving Turtle Creek
we settle into a rhythm—
paddling fast enough

to move forward,
but not so fast it hurts my arm.
Rose could go faster, I know,

but she keeps time,
gliding lazily through
the deep blue water

as though our company
is all she really wants.
Every so often, I'll stick my hand

over the kayak's side
and Rose will nudge it.
Without words, we say,

I'll miss you,
I love you,
thank you
for being my friend.

ON THE RIVER

With every mile
the Neuse brings us something
new to catch our breath:
a line of pelicans who soar and dive;
a tall white sailboat
that seems to almost fly.
There's not much traffic—
only the occasional crab boat
with a waterman collecting his pots,
or a fishing dory idling by the shore.
But the quiet river
is vibrantly alive around us.

Two hours
after leaving Turtle Creek,
we paddle into the middle
of a whole school
of strangely thin, finned fish—
hundreds, maybe thousands
leaping from the water,
there and gone
so fast I'd miss it if I blinked,
making only the tiniest *glop*
as they sink back underneath.

"Needlefish," Daddy breathes
after studying the mysterious creatures.
"Never seen this many."
The long dark bodies
ripple in and out, in and out
in every direction—
behind us, before us, to either side.
"I didn't know they could even school
this big," Daddy says.

I push the button
on my walkie-talkie and ask
Dr. Zhao, maybe two hundred yards
behind us, "Are you seeing this?"
"Remarkable," she crackles back.
"How's Rose taking it?"

I look to the water, where Rose
is tearing through the school
with joyous delight,
scattering needlefish right and left.
She dives and leaps and dives again,
her whole enormous body
wriggling with pleasure.
Maybe I'd feel the same if, one day,
I found a sidewalk covered
in inches of chocolate bars.

"I think it might be hard
to get her away from this," I say
into the radio,
and hear Dr. Zhao's tinny laugh.
And in this moment,
with Rose gamboling through the water
like it's Christmas morning
and the sun on my skin
and the burn in my arm from
all this paddling—

I'm not sure I've ever, ever felt
just how wonderful it is
to be alive.

LUNCH

Dr. Zhao says
we might as well let Rose eat her fill,
        and since it's almost noon
Daddy pulls out our sandwiches, too.
        I eat my warm, melty PB&J
and then trail my hand in the water
        to get the sticky off.
I wish I could just jump in—
        join Rose,
let the cool river wash away
        the sweat and grime
that coats my skin. The sun is hot
        and bright, right overhead,
and I long to feel the water all around me.
        My Press'n Sealed arm
is the worst part—the plastic holds
        the heat in, oven-like,
sweat pooling underneath,
        itching at my skin.
If it weren't for cystic fibrosis—
        if I didn't have a PICC line—
I'd definitely dive in.
        And even though I'm glad

I'm here, and glad that what we're doing
      might save Rose's life—
I *hate* that CF took that away from me,
      the chance to feel
the cold silk water on my skin, to swim
      again with Rose.

      The last two weeks
have been a patchwork of lucky and unlucky,
      fortunate and not-so-much.
But for the first time maybe ever,
      when anger and unfairness
simmer inside me, whispering of all the things
      I've lost because of my CF,
I don't try to tamp them down again.
      I don't count my blessings
or remind myself of all the ways
      it could be worse.
I don't think about the fact that I'm
      one of the lucky ones.
I just let those messy feelings come,
      wash over me like waves,
trusting that, like waves, they'll pass.

THE SECOND HALF

After lunch
things get harder.
My arm hurts,
an ache
that spreads
from my shoulder
to my fingertips,
and I stop paddling.
The sun is
unrelenting
on my skin.
Where my sweat
has dried,
salt sparkles—
the salt
CF pulls out of me,
leaving me
feeling faint
and crabby.
Daddy gives me
more salt pills,
reminds me
to drink water

or Gatorade
every half hour
at least.

But it isn't only
the heat
and the tiredness
that make
the second half
hard—
it's knowing
that each mile
we paddle
takes us closer
to the moment
we say
      goodbye
    to
        Rose.

WIDE, WIDE RIVER

The farther downstream we get,
the more the river widens.
An hour or so after we stop for lunch
we come to a place where the water is so wide
it seems to stretch on either side of us
forever—endless sparkling blue
almost as far as I can see.
Daddy pulls out the GPS app on his phone
and measures the width,
says, "Whoa, it's almost five miles."
I wonder if Rose, who's swum away
to investigate
a line of crab-pot buoys by the shore,
can sense it—our proximity to the Sound.
We're more than halfway
to our destination.
If I didn't know Daddy would say *no way*,
I'd dip a finger in the water,
taste it to see
if it seems saltier than Turtle Creek.
When Rose comes back from nosing at the crab pots,
I splash her with my hand

and she splashes back, and I wonder
if *she* can taste the salt
and if she knows it means
she's almost home.

REMEMBERING

Now that I can't paddle much
I pull my phone out
and snap pictures:
photos of the Neuse,
the trees, the sun,
of Rose, still swimming
faithfully alongside us, as smart
and loyal as any dog.

With every hour that passes
I know we're coming closer
to the end. And if I can't
stop this trip from ending,
can't make the twisting
in my chest at the thought
of saying goodbye go away—
at least I can make sure
I've got pictures to remember.

DADDY

The farther we go, the quieter we get,
me and Daddy.
But as the sun finally goes behind a cloud
and Rose spins and dives in the water,
just for fun,
and a flock of seagulls passes overhead,
I think how glad I am
that it's me and Daddy here.
That Daddy—with his strong arms
and his stillness,
his laughter and his care,
his brilliant brain that holds so much
about lungs and hearts—
is the one tucked behind me,
pulling us through the water.
I wonder if this is how Liana feels
when they go on trips together,
and under my breath
I hum a bit of "Row, Row, Row Your Boat."
Rose swims up beside us,
almost like she can hear my humming,
and I reach a hand to her,
wondering about *her* daddy, *her* mama,

if she has any Lianas of her own
out there in the big blue world.
Can she feel their presence now,
maybe just a few miles from where we are,

calling,
            calling,
                        calling her home?

ENDINGS

I've never liked endings.
Maybe that's one reason
I like poetry sometimes
better than stories—
because poems don't end
the same way stories do,
but slither inside your bones
to whisper and breathe.
And when Daddy says
his GPS has us almost there,
where Neuse meets Sound—
my stomach clenches,
my arm aches worse,
the burn of tears pricks
behind my eyelids.
Not ready not ready not ready,
I think, because even though
I know Turtle Creek
is no place for a dolphin,
even though I know Rose
needs her pod as much
as I need mine—

I'm not ready to see her
swim into the distance.

Not ready for an ending.

GOODBYES ARE HARD

I know we've reached our destination
when up ahead, the north side of the river
falls away, and as far as eyes can see
there's just water, water, water.
At first, when Daddy stops paddling
in the middle of the wide, wide river
Rose doesn't notice.
She keeps going, rolling through the water
until a minute passes, and she turns
and swims back to us.
When she reaches the kayak
she lifts her head up and squirts a great
stream of water at us,
like she's saying, *What's wrong with you?*
Don't you see the mysterious beautiful water,
waiting to be explored?
She circles us a few times, then nudges
the bow of our boat,
just enough to make it rock.

Behind us, the pop and thrum of the motor
on Dr. Zhao's boat cuts out
as she catches up and waits a few yards away.

She and Esteban and Madison
are all lined up at the console, eyes on Rose.
"This is the hard part,"
Dr. Zhao calls over, close enough
we don't need walkie-talkies.
"Getting Rose to keep going into the Sound.
We'll track her, and in a few days
I'll take a team to visit her,
make sure she's showing signs of improvement.
But right now—
right now, it's all up to her."

Rose nudges our bow again.
"Dang it, dolphin," Daddy says. "Stop!"
I imagine what might happen if the boat rocks
just a *little* too far—
Daddy and I splashing in,
water enfolding my plastic-wrapped arm,
all the things Mama was afraid of.
Rose stops bumping us, retreats a foot or two,
but doesn't go farther.
She lifts her melon head up, out of the water,
ink-black eyes on us.

I take a deep breath.
I feel the air fill my lungs all the way down
to the bottom. I don't let myself stop

or flinch away, even when it makes me cough,
even when I flash right back
to last week's hemoptysis
and anxiety zaps through me.
I hold out my hand to Rose,
and she comes and lets me rub my fingers
over her soft silver skin.

"Goodbyes are hard," I say, voice quiet,
like it's only me and her, back at my dock.
"Aren't they, girl?
I'm going to miss you.
Turtle Creek will feel so empty."
I close my eyes and try to *listen*—
let the lap of the water
and the call of the gulls
and the distant motor of a boat
all disappear. And once I do, I can hear her—
not exactly with my ears, but with my heart.

> *Confusion*
> *Exhaustion*
> *Fear.*

I see the whole thing suddenly through *her* eyes:
the long journey she must have taken
weeks ago, to end up in our creek;

the heaviness that settled into her lungs—
just like mine.
The unfamiliar setting, dirty water,
lonely, wandering days.
Rose's feelings are so big I almost cannot breathe.
I think of the picture she showed me before,
her pod leaping from silver water.
"I bet you miss them," I say, "right?"
A wave of grief rolls over me
and Rose makes that sad, keening sound again.

I say, "You have to keep on going."
The words tear out of me
like a bandage ripped off skin.
"They're waiting for you out there."
I look downstream, at the sparkle of the Sound,
so broad it almost feels
like the sea itself.
Can Rose find her pod?
Will she try?
I close my eyes again,
picture Rose swimming forward fast and sure.
I hold that image in my mind
as clear as clear can be
and try, somehow, to make Rose see it, too.

She clicks and croons,
bumping my hand with her head,
then splashes me the tiniest bit,
her perpetual grin as wide as ever—
and then, between one breath and the next
she is sinking back down under the water,
circling our kayak one last time,
nodding her head at me just like a human might,
and with one mighty muscled push
she is

                        P   I
              A   N
        E   G
L

away from us, her silver body shining
in the sunlight, swimming strong and swift
into the wide wonderful water of the Sound
her fin rolling in and out, in and out,
just like the day Liana first saw her in our creek.

WHAT I KNOW ABOUT PENNY ROONEY, PART 4

Small girl
all bones and points

who can be
brave and wonderful

who can
believe impossible things

who can learn
how to hold on and let go.

NEVER ALONE

From behind
I feel Daddy's hand
rest on my shoulder,
warm and soft,
and I realize
I'm crying, salty tears
carving tracks
down my sweat-stained face,
crying like I haven't
since the last time
the home health nurse
came to draw my blood.
"Goodbyes are hard,"
Daddy says, echoing my words
back to me.
"Endings hurt,
no matter how right they are.
But you did a brave,
amazing thing, Penny.
That dolphin
maybe owes her life
to you.
But she isn't gone

forever. No matter what
happens, she'll always be a part
of you, and you a part
of her. That's how friendship
works, honey."

I scrub at my eyes
and feel the teary hiccups
slow, calm settling
across my skin.
I think of how I heard Rose call
in those early morning hours
even though I was in bed
and she was down
in Turtle Creek.
I think about the way
we swam together,
the way
she let me rub her head,
the way we somehow
speak without a language.
Daddy's right:
no distance can cut
the golden thread of love
I wove with Rose.

And suddenly I think
of Cricket,
of the moving boxes
piled in her house,
the day her mama circled
on the calendar
and wrote *MOVE OUT*
in big red letters.
Thinking of Cricket gone
feels like somebody's prying
at my rib cage,
a pain so sharp and hot
I wish I could throw it in the sea.
But maybe this, too,
is a lesson Rose has taught me—
that no distance
can part Cricket'n'Penny,
no move can end
our sisterhood.

Right at that moment
the phone tucked into my life jacket
buzzes, and I see
I've got a message
from Sophia.
Sophia—the friend

I've never had but always needed.
The one who knows exactly
all the ways CF
can push and pull.
The friend I thought I couldn't have.

And that's the thing
that makes my heart almost
e x p l o d e
with understanding.
We're all connected—
Rose—Cricket—Sophia
and the other CFers I've found
on Instagram.
Because no matter
how lonely I might feel
in the small hours of the night—
no matter how far
I might be from
the people I love—

I am joined to them
just as much as Rose was still
joined to her pod,
even when she was lost
in my backyard.

No matter the distance
no matter the struggle
I am *never* alone.

HEADING HOME

All traces of my tears have dried
by the time Daddy and I pull up at the dock
where Mama and Liana wait.
With Rose gone,
Dr. Zhao revved her motor
and putted right behind us.
Once we're all standing on the warm wood
and Daddy's hefted the kayak
out of the water,
Dr. Zhao asks, "May I hug you, Penny?"
She's smiling bigger than I've ever seen her
as she wraps her arms around me
and pulls me close.
"You're an extraordinary young woman,
Penny Rooney," she says
when she's pulled away.
"It's been a long time
since I met someone with such a love
for dolphins as you have.
Give me a call when you're in college, okay?
We can always use an intern."
I don't really know if marine biology
is in my future, but I tell Dr. Zhao thanks

and high-five Madison and Esteban
and wave from the back seat of the pickup
as Mama pulls onto the highway.
Liana's in the back with me,
and I show her all the photos I took—
of us, of Rose, the sun-kissed river.
She exclaims over them all,
says, "I'm going to be
jealous until I die"
(which seems pretty fair
after all the years I've envied her).
Daddy hands me
a loaded nebulizer and my vest
and I do a breathing treatment
right there, in the car.
Now that I'm out of the kayak,
no paddle in my hands,
the sun shielded from my back,
exhaustion steamrolls over me
and when my treatment finally finishes,
I slump against the door of the truck
and sleep the whole way home.

LATER

Monday afternoon
oozes by, a haze
of catnaps and treatments.
A home health nurse comes
to change my PICC dressing tape
(OUCH)
and draw more blood
(DOUBLE OUCH)
to make sure my antibiotic
dose is right.
Cricket comes over
after school
and when she walks through
the door, I hug her
tighter than I maybe ever have,
the achy, empty place
Rose left in my heart
throbbing hard.
Cricket scrolls through
my photos, chattering
in amazement
at the magical journey
that already feels half-real.

Did we really do that,
Daddy and me?
Did we really paddle fifteen miles
down one of
America's widest rivers
with a dolphin alongside?
Did we really watch her
splash and dive
through thousands of needlefish?
The memories are muddled now,
like something from another life.

ANOTHER DREAM

That night
I dream:
sunlight sparkles
on water silver-blue
as a dolphin
with a tracker tag
in her dorsal
leaps and leaps again,
surrounded
by a dozen other
dolphins.

Rose
   has found
      her pod.

HEALING

The rest of my week is slow and empty
now that Rose is gone.
I wake up every day feeling just
a *little* better than the day before,
and when she looks at me, Mama's smile
is as bright as the sun.
I cough less every day,
and Daddy says, *You're healing great, Pen.*

But I'm not ready for school quite yet.
"We'll try a half day back
when your IVs are done next week,"
Mama says. "Start slow. Build up."
I message @yoursaltysophia and ask,
*Have you ever missed a bunch of school
because of your CF?*
She tells me about a time
a few years back when she got so sick
she was out of school for a whole month.

There are less than five weeks left
of the school year, and then
Cricket moves away.

Every day that passes is another bus ride,
another homeroom, another lunchtime
I could be with Cricket
if I went back to school.
Talking to Sophia doesn't take away
the pain when I think
of all I'm missing, but
it makes the hurt a little softer,
knowing I'm not the only one
who sometimes misses out thanks to
these sixty-five stinking roses.

MY POEM

On Thursday,
after working all week
on my poem
for Ms. Berman's poetry slam,
I type up the words
I wrote into my poetry notebook,
log into her Google Classroom,
paste the stanzas in,
hold my breath,
and hit Send.

As I press that green button
a good feeling tingles
in my fingertips,
bubbles down me
to my toes. I don't know
if the committee will choose
my poem or not.

But I know more
about Penny Rooney
than I did three weeks ago
and for now, that is enough.

BACK AT THE DOCK

The next Monday, we have a special dinner
to celebrate getting my PICC line out
after finishing
my fourteen-day IV course.
Cricket's family comes
and we eat in the backyard,
ears full of cicada song.
It's weird, having my arm back to normal—
no tape to crinkle when I move,
no achy tube shoved up in my vein.
It's weird, too, that I hardly cough;
that when I take a big breath
nothing crackles deep within my lungs.

After dinner we all walk down to the creek.
Daddy and Mama and Cricket's parents
set up chairs on the grass
and Cricket's brothers skip stones
into the water.
Cricket and I sit on the edge of the dock,
heads together, shoulders touching.
Liana puts a Taylor Swift playlist on
and I dip my toes into the creek
while the music washes over us

and it feels like a perfect end to a perfect
night, like everything in these
wild three weeks has led me to this moment.
When Liana's favorite song starts playing,
she and I aren't the only ones
to sing along—everybody does,
from Daddy down
to Cricket's smallest brother.
My lungs feel strong and full of air
as I belt the chorus.

I close my eyes, and I swear
I can see against the darkness of my eyelids
a golden thread spooling from my chest,
spiderwebbing out in every direction—
one tendril hooks to Cricket,
another rides the stream of music to Liana,
more float on the wind behind me
to join to Mama and Daddy.
One swirls through the creek water and disappears
into the distance, and somehow
I know it's Rose there, on the other end.
Some fly high, hitch on clouds,
tether me to @yoursaltysophia and @cfmaddy,
to all the people out there just like me
living under this same blue sky.

I don't feel so much
like a blank slate anymore.
Today, I am a fresh page
in a well-loved notebook—
a notebook full
of things I've learned about myself
but with plenty of blank space left
to hold all these golden threads.
Because what I know about Penny Rooney
is that she is different
for being friends with Cricket, sisters with Liana,
daughter to Elizabeth and Steve.
She's been changed by a dolphin named Rose
with silver skin and a permanent smile,
and even though she hasn't known them long
her new CF friends
are already written on her heart.

Maybe I don't know yet
ALL the things that make me *me*—
but sitting here on the dock with the evening breeze
around me, singing aloud with my blood sister
and my heart sister
and my parents—
the not-knowing feels less like emptiness
and more like thrilling possibility.

One Month Later

ON STAGE

The spotlight is bright and hot
on the middle school stage
as I step up to the microphone.
My hands are a little sweaty
and without thinking,
I rub the tiny moon-shaped scar
in the crook of my elbow,
where the PICC line
threaded through my veins.
and everyone's parents and siblings
and aunts and uncles,
a whole sea of faces floating
hazy in the auditorium.

I close my eyes
and think of that day in the kayak
with Rose, the sun all around us.
I take a deep, slow breath.
And when I speak, my voice is strong
and doesn't tremble
as I read my poem out loud.

WHAT I KNOW ABOUT PENNY ROONEY

This is what I know:
I could write a thousand poems about Penny Rooney
and still never peel back all the layers
there are to me.

A small girl, all bones and points—
but mighty. Strong. True.

The kind of person
who believes in miracles
and impossible things, who knows
what it feels like
to swim beside a creature made of joy.

A friend, a sister, a daughter,
defined by all those things—
but also
just
defined by being me.

A girl born with something different,
something extra
deep inside each breath,

sixty-five purple roses
that grow within my skin.

Someone who understands
the beauty of an empty page—
the promise
of a life that's not yet written.

Lucky and unlucky,
brave and yet afraid—

I could write a thousand poems about Penny Rooney
and still never peel back all the layers
there are to me.

It's a good thing I've got
a whole big life to do it in.

AUTHOR'S NOTE

All my books are close to my heart, but none of them are as deeply personal as *No Matter the Distance*. Just like Penny, I was diagnosed with cystic fibrosis as a baby, after becoming very sick and almost dying. Doctors' appointments, handfuls of daily pills, and breathing treatments were a normal part of my childhood.

When I was born, the median life expectancy for a person with CF was around twenty-five years old, and many CF patients didn't live into adulthood. Although I was very aware of the fact that I was "lucky" and "healthy" for a CFer, I still struggled with the tough parts of my disease—like nights of coughing, constant stomach pain, the severe phobia of needles that came with regular blood draws, and isolated hospital stays.

Growing up with CF was a lonely experience. When I was eleven, researchers discovered that CF patients could infect one another with their dangerous bacteria, and my CF center stopped allowing patients to meet each other in real life. Long before the COVID-19 pandemic began, CF patients were experts at social distancing (what our community calls "the six-foot rule"), wearing masks in public spaces, and connecting virtually instead of face-to-face. Today, many of my closest friends are other CFers I have never met in person.

While I was blessed with loving parents and a supportive CF team, I often received the message from the adults in my life that I just needed to focus on how lucky I was rather than on my panic about needles or how scary nights alone in the hospital could be. Like Penny, I was often reminded of the stories of other people with CF who had it worse than I did—those who were hospitalized more frequently, had been listed for double-lung transplants, or died young.

These severe cases of cystic fibrosis are also what most media portrayals have focused on—and while it is still heartbreakingly common for a preteen or teen with CF to have dozens of hospital stays and health crises under their belt, and many CF patients still die far too young, the prognosis for CF has greatly improved since I was born. In 2021, the median life expectancy for kids born in the United States with CF hit fifty years old for the first time. In *No Matter the Distance*, I wanted to tell the story of a CF patient a lot like me: one who had been spared from the most dramatic and life-threatening aspects of the disease but who still struggled with the difficult moments that even "mild" CF can bring.

Many children who live with serious illnesses are raised in a culture that encourages positivity and inspiration at all costs. With Penny's story, I wanted to show that it is normal and okay to have a hard time with your personal challenges— even if they're not as severe as they *could* be. I hope that *No Matter the Distance* can show another facet of the complex, variable illness that is cystic fibrosis.

To learn about CF, you can visit the United States Cystic Fibrosis Foundation at www.cff.org. In addition to educating about cystic fibrosis, the CFF raises money for research and has been responsible for investing in medications that have dramatically increased the life expectancy of people with CF.

Like it was for Penny, my primary way of connecting with the CF community is through social media. On Instagram, you can visit the official CFF account @cf_foundation. Many local CFF chapters also have Instagram accounts, such as @cffoundationcarolinas—the CFF chapter for Penny's region—or @cff_oregon, my local chapter. On my personal Instagram account, @cindybaldwinbooks, I frequently share details about what my life with CF is like. There are also several Instagram hashtags that can help you find more examples of what a CF life looks like. My favorites are #cysticfibrosis, #cfirl, and #sixtyfiveroses. (Please have a grown-up help you when exploring social media hashtags!)

Love,
Cindy Baldwin

ACKNOWLEDGMENTS

Living with cystic fibrosis is complicated, requiring community support and a team of medical specialists. Being an author and a mom with CF is even trickier, and I couldn't do it without the help of many people!

First and foremost, I want to thank my parents, Russ and Cindy Ray. Raising a kid with a demanding, life-shortening disease is not a task for the faint of heart, and I will forever be grateful for the balance my parents gave me as they taught me how to respect and care for my health while still dreaming big.

My siblings are a precious part of my life. Although their lives have all been impacted by my CF, they have surrounded me with deep love and friendship. I'm also grateful for the support I've received from my in-laws on both sides of the family.

My husband, Mahon, has been my best friend and biggest cheerleader for fifteen years. He has been there for every late-night cry, hospital stay, and hemoptysis. My daughter, Kate, helped me run IV medications when she was still a toddler and has sat with me through thousands of breathing treatments, even when she *really* wanted me to play a game with her instead. Kate was my first beta reader for *No Matter the Distance*, and she gave me careful and wonderful feedback.

I could never have reached such a distinguished age with CF without the help of many medical professionals. I'm grateful for the care I've received throughout my life from teams at the University of North Carolina, Duke University, and the University of Utah. I'm especially grateful for Dr. Judith Voynow; Barbara McLurkin, NP; Bill Taub, LCSW; Dr. Theodore Liou; Jennifer Kinsfather, RN; and Steve LaFortune, RT. In addition to helping me stay healthy, my current care team at OHSU—Virginia Satcher, NP; Dr. Aaron Trimble; Dr. Gopal Allada; Ash Swift, RN; Kim Keeling, RT; Cori Muirhead, PharmD; Daniella Gardner, RD; and Carly Michelz, RD—have become treasured friends and wonderful champions of my books. (Aaron, thanks for signing off on Penny kayaking with a PICC line!) My fellow CFer Willem Wery deserves a mention as a brilliant coconspirator on our work with the OHSU CF Clinic Quality Improvement team.

I've been a part of the online CF community since I was a teenager. To my CF friends: you have seen me through many challenges, and I am grateful for each one of you. Megan Murray, James Lawlor, Sydna Marshall, and Rachael Haig gave wonderful feedback on different parts of this book. My

TeensWithCF, Cyster Friends, and CF Mummies, I love you. Thanks to every friend who answered the many strange research questions I came up with, like "Have any of you ever kayaked with a PICC line?!"

I'm grateful for the feedback and cheerleading of many critique partners, including Shannon Cooley, Amanda Rawson Hill, Sarah Allen, Ashley Martin, Juliana Brandt, Rosalyn Eves, Jamie Pacton, and all of #TeamMascaraTracks.

My agent, Elizabeth Harding, was an advocate of this story through many different iterations, and her faith and steadfastness helped me to figure out what I most wanted to say with this book. My editor, Alexandra Cooper, has an uncanny ability to give feedback that reaches right into the heart of my story and makes me say, "Why didn't I think of that?!" Illustrator Zeina Shareef created a cover illustration that is beautiful beyond my wildest dreams. Others at Quill Tree Books who were instrumental in bringing this book into the world include Allison Weintraub, Mikayla Lawrence, and Valerie Shea.

Finally, I am unspeakably grateful for the many tireless advocates who have dedicated their lives to improving the outcome for CFers. In 2012, I began taking a groundbreaking medication called a CFTR modulator—the first treatment in history that helps to correct a genetic defect at the cellular level. Because of that medication and its successors, I've been able to realize my dreams of becoming a mom and a published author. I owe my life to the people who have helped in the discovery of these therapies, including everyone who has donated to the Cystic Fibrosis Foundation to help fund the development of new, lifesaving treatments for people like me.